White Pine

My Year as a Lumberjack and a River Rat

by

Caroline Akervik

F & I
by Melange Books

Published by
Fire and Ice
A Young Adult Imprint of Melange Books, LLC
White Bear Lake, MN 55110
www.fireandiceya.com

White Pine ~ Copyright © 2014 by Caroline Akervik

ISBN: 978-1-61235-826-0

Cover Art and Illustrations by Julie Schaller
Cover Layout and Design: Caroline Andrus

Dedication

For Andy, Aslan, Charlotte, and Johan.

This story was inspired by our adventures geocaching one summer not so long ago when you kids were much smaller. On that particular day, we'd learned that old brick building we passed so many times on the way to the hockey rink had actually once been a lumber company office. We talked about the history of the area and what you'd learned at the Chippewa Valley Museum during your third grade field trip there. One of you told me that I should I write a lumberjack story. I wish I'd managed to get it done sooner, but children grow more quickly than books (as C.S. Lewis pointed out). One day, I hope you'll pick up this little book and remember our adventures on that long ago, sunshiny day.

Johan, you said there weren't any books with your name in it. White Pine aims at correcting that little oversight.

Andy, without your love and your patience with my reading, writing and day dreaming, this story and all of the others wouldn't be possible.

This book is meant for girls and boys, but especially for those boys who don't care for fantasy but who want action and adventure in what they read.

Please excuse any errors or historical inaccuracies in this book. This is a work of fiction and my goal was to capture the spirit and the heart of the lumberjack era in Wisconsin.

Chapter One
~ A Visitor ~

I never planned on working in the pineries. Ma and Pa agreed that the best thing for all of us Andersen kids was to go to school, where we could learn to be good Americans. That was real important to Pa, being the son of immigrants.

Pa said that's why he'd come here to the United States from Norway, to make things better for his family. Like all the other lumberjacks, he worked the pineries in the winter, 'cause the logs needed to be cut and ready for the snowmelt. In the spring, the rivers ran high and could carry the logs down to the mills in the sawdust cities like Eau Claire, where we lived. In the summer, Pa worked at the mill just down the road from the house we rented. He worked real hard so that one day we could have a farm of our own. Ma and Pa had been talking about it for so long that it didn't seem like it would ever happen. And then, Pa got hurt.

On the morning that I told my teacher, Mr. Watters, that I was leaving school, I waltzed in there like I was the president of the

United States of America. I didn't even sit at my desk. I just went right up to the front of the schoolhouse, to Mr. Watters.

"Today's my last day, sir."

He didn't pay me no mind. He was too busy looking at what the Nelson twins were doing in the front row—pounding each other, as usual.

"Boys," he said. "That's quite enough of that."

They didn't listen. They never did.

I cleared my throat. "Mr. Watters—"

"Take your seat, Sevy," he cut me off. "Bob and Will, if I have to come over there."

"Mr. Watters." This time, I touched his arm to get his attention. That stopped him. "I'm leaving school for good. I'm going to the pineries, taking my Pa's place."

He eyeballed me. Mr. Watters was young, blond, skinny, and kind of a nervous type, but he was a decent fella. He'd come from out East and he dressed sort of fancy for out here in Wisconsin, but he wasn't snooty or anything like that.

"You're leaving school?" He said it like I was planning on killin' somebody.

"I have to. My Pa can't work. He broke his leg."

Mr. Watters' brow knit—like he was thinking hard about this. He pursed his lips. "Now's not the time for this discussion. Please take your seat, Sevy. Bob, Will, that is quite enough."

I'd told him. He just wasn't listening real well. So, I walked out. What else could I do? On my way, I winked at Hugh MacLean, my best friend. His eyes were huge, like he couldn't believe what I was doing. Most of the other kids watched me jealously, no doubt wishing they were the ones doing the walking out.

Mr. Watters came to our house that night. Us Andersens were just setting down for supper. Mrs. Engelstad, one of my ma's lady friends from church, had made kroppkakor for us. Folks had been bringing us grub all week, since Pa got hurt. Kroppkakor was one of my favorite suppers. I always put the butter thick on the dumplings. And nothing tasted better than when you bit through them to the salt pork.

Ma had already brought Pa his dinner in the bedroom and the rest of us had just sat down at the table when someone knocked at the door. We looked around at each other. No one generally came by at supper time.

"Are you going to make me get up on my broken leg?" Pa growled from the other room.

I glanced at my ma, who just shook her head. She looked tired, worried, too. She sighed, wiped her hands on her apron and went to the door. The rest of us, me, Peter, my brother, and my little sister, Marta, just stayed where we were, sitting on the benches at the table.

When she opened the door, we saw Mr. Watters standing there. He held his hat in his hands. "Mrs. Andersen?"

"Yes."

He glanced in at us. "I apologize for interrupting your supper, but could I get a word? There's a matter I need to discuss with you."

"Sevy," Ma turned a sharp eye on me. "Have you been causing trouble at school?"

"No, Ma."

"No, he hasn't," Mr. Watters agreed. He looked nervous and I didn't blame him none for that. Ma was a tall woman, a good head and shoulders taller than Mr. Watters, and she had a way about her that didn't brook no nonsense. "But there is a matter of some concern that arose today."

"Come in, Mr. Watters." Ma stepped to the side.

"Who's out there?" Pa demanded, his voice thick and angry. Maybe he'd been drinking some of the whiskey that Ma had tucked away for special occasions. Don't get me wrong, Pa wasn't a drunk. But he was hurting in a serious way with his leg all busted up as it was.

"School teacher, Gus. There ain't no trouble. Or there better not be," Ma spoke the last part direct to me.

I just shook my head. What could I say? Ma usually smiled and laughed a lot, but since Pa had broke his leg just a few days before, she'd been troubled. She'd been growling at us kids near as much as Pa.

"Please take a seat, Mr. Watters," she directed him to the wooden bench by nine-year-old Marta. "Have you had your supper yet?"

Us kids listened close at that. We all wanted as much kroppkakor as possible. We didn't much like the idea of sharing.

"Thank you. I haven't, but—"

"Peter, get another a plate."

Watters waved a hand. "That won't be necessary. I'll be here for just a few minutes. It's about Sevy. Today, he informed me that he will not be returning to school."

I saw the muscle clench in the corner of Ma's jaw. She picked up her fork real careful, put a piece of dumpling in her mouth and chewed it slow. Still, she didn't look up at Mr. Watters.

I knew she didn't like me leaving school one bit. I'd heard her arguing with Pa over it every night, and he didn't like it none, either. But there didn't seem to be any way around it.

"Pa broke his leg at the mill. A big log rolled on him. Now Sevy has to go to the pineries instead." Peter spit it all out in a rush. He always talked too much without thinking.

"Peter," I scolded. Mr. Watters had no right knowing our family business.

"Is this true?" Watter questioned with a disapproving frown.

Ma looked him right in the eye. "Mr. Watters, we always tell our children that schooling is real important, so that they can do something with their lives. But then this accident happened." She paused, leaned forward and spoke softly. "We're hopin that Gus, my husband Gustav, will be on his feet by summer."

"But why does the boy have to sit out the vast majority of the school year? Sevy has a fine mind and he's a talented writer. He could go far with his education."

I blushed at the praise. Mr. Watters had never said anything nice about me like that before.

Ma answered, "Gus works in the mill in the summer and fall and in the pineries in the winter."

"I still don't understand. How does this impact your son's education?"

Figured he wouldn't. We'd all heard that Watters came from a wealthy family somewhere out east.

"Sevy has to work, so we don't have to move to the poor house," Marta piped up.

"Children, that's enough," Ma corrected.

"Yeah, hush," I said, giving my little sister the evil eye. "You shouldn't talk like that in front of folk who ain't family."

Mr. Watters wasn't a fool, and he looked at all of us seated around the table. He nodded slowly. "Hmm, yes." He cleared his throat. "Well then, Sevy, I'll look forward to seeing you next fall. This has been a pleasant visit, but I must be on my way. Marta and Peter, I'll see you in school tomorrow. Mrs. Andersen, thank you for your hospitality."

Ma set her napkin on the table and moved to stand up.

"No please, don't get up," Watters declared as he placed his hat back on his head. "I'll see myself out. My greetings and good wishes to your husband." He stood there for a minute, eyeing me as if he wanted to say something else but couldn't think of how to put it.

I don't know what took hold of me, but then I smarted off, "You won't see me back in that schoolhouse. I may like workin' up north."

"Sevy," Ma snapped and I knew that I'd get it later. As for Watters, he just looked like I'd slapped him one.

"Have a good evening." He sorta bowed his head to Ma, then left.

Funny, I'd always thought that smartin' off to him would feel good. But it didn't. I felt kind of guilty, that school teacher had looked right sad when I told him I wouldn't be back.

Chapter Two
~ Preparations ~

I wasn't supposed to head north until the weather began to cool. So, for two more weeks, I stayed at home and helped my ma. Pa was like a bear with a thorn in his paw. But when I wasn't working hard, I was dreamin' about what it was going to be like up in the Northwoods, so I didn't mind much. On a Saturday just before I was set to leave, Ma gave me some money to buy some necessaries for myself for the winter.

I made a point of going by the MacLean Tavern on Barstow. The tavern, a narrow store front, was owned by Hugh's uncle, but Hugh worked there a lot. Sure enough, as the door opened, letting in fresh air, I glimpsed him inside sweeping the floor. Hugh was a tall skinny kid with light reddish hair and green eyes. His folks were from Ireland, and the Irish and the Norwegian folk in Eau Claire didn't tend to mix much. But Hugh was my best friend and had been since we were eight years old when we'd met at school.

"Hey Hugh, want to do some shopping with me?" I called

out, feeling real important.

His eyes got big and he almost dropped his broom. *"Dia duit. Let me check with my uncle."*

Mr. MacLean said Hugh had to finish up his cleaning chores. With me helping him, though, we were done in no time.

"You think that we'll have enough left over for some penny candy?" Hugh asked as we headed down the street. We stayed off the wooden boards of the sidewalk, leaving it for the ladies and the rich gents who cared about getting their boots dirty. It had rained the night before, and the sawdust which was always all over everything had soaked the water up and now stuck to our shoes and pants. Eau Claire had a well-earned reputation as a sawdust city. You could even taste the pine in the air.

"Guess who's been asking after you at school," Hugh teased.

I didn't want to seem too interested, that would be just what Hugh wanted and it ain't the Norwegian way. I might have been only half Norwegian—my Ma was born in the United States and her folks were from Sweden to start—but we were not like the Irish folks. They'd tell anyone just about anything.

"Dunno," I lied.

"A girl," he said, "and a pretty one."

"Your sister Margaret?"

He punched me in the arm hard for that. "Meg's eighteen and engaged to the baker's assistant. You know that. This particular girl has been asking how come you ain't at school no more."

That got my attention. There was one particular girl who'd caught my eye. Adelaide was her name and she had thick, shiny blond hair and the bluest eyes you ever saw. I don't think we'd ever said more to each other than "Hello." But sometimes when I was answering one of Mr. Watters' questions or reciting in class, I'd look over at her and then she'd blush and look down at her book. I thought maybe she liked me, a little, too.

"Carrie Winters. Why she stopped me just the other day and asked what you were up to."

I turned to glare at my friend. "Carrie Winters," I repeated incredulously. "She's as mean and cantankerous as a mule."

"She has a twinkle in her eye for you."

"No, she doesn't. You're just making fun." Hugh wanted me to beg him, but I wasn't going to give him the satisfaction. He wouldn't be able to keep it from me – he was just bustin' to tell me. We strolled down Menomonie Street until we arrived at Whiteside's General Store. I swung the door wide and gestured him in.

Whiteside's was one of those stores that had just about anything a fella could think of wanting. Whenever Ma or Pa came in, they were always looking for something specific, a tool or utensil, maybe some cloth. Then, us kids would wander through the aisles, taking it all in, our eyes wide with wonder. There were smells in there, too: nutmeg and ginger, tobacco, and the ever present pine. Whiteside's had so many things that I wanted, like store-bought fishing rods. Hugh and I used ones we'd made for fishing the Chippewa River. For the longest time, my sister had had her eye on a china doll and my brother, on a rifle he wanted to use for turkey hunting.

But this time, going in was different – I was an actual customer with money to buy things. I sauntered right up to the counter where they stocked the penny candy and said, "Where do you keep the gear for the lumberjacks?"

"Back up against the wall, son," Augie Whiteside, a big man

with a huge black handlebar mustache directed me. "You're looking for the Nor and Blum goods. What size is your father?"

From behind me, I heard Hugh snort.

"We're shopping for me, not for my Pa. I'm going to be a lumberjack with the Daniel Shaw Lumber Company." I stood up straight then so that he could see how tall I was. I was taller than most men, had been since I was twelve, and now at fourteen I wasn't scrawny like Hugh. I'd always been thicker set and strong, but Ma said I had a "baby-face" that made me look young. I took after my Ma with her blond hair and brown eyes. I wished I took more after Pa, though. He was big, strong as an ox and his face was tough looking.

Mr. Whiteside eyed me up and down skeptically. "Most boys your age at the lumber camps work as cookees. They need different gear than the jacks. You sure you're not signed up to be a cookee?"

"No, I'm gonna be a sawyer." I didn't dare to voice my real ambition which was to be a top loader. Everyone in a sawdust city like Eau Claire knew that the top loaders were the royalty of the logging camp, and there was no chance that any self-respecting Push would let a wet-behind-the-ears fourteen year old do that job.

"A sawyer, all right then." He shook his head. "Well, let's get you outfitted, young man. You'll need a union suit, some wool shirts, pants, socks, caps, and a heavy coat—unless you already have one of those?"

For a moment, I wished I could say that I would take all of it, even the coat. Ma had told me to pick out what I needed and had given me the money for it. But then I pictured Marta, Peter, Pa, and, most of all, Ma, and how tired her face had been looking lately. She was taking in mending for some of the men who worked at the mill, but that didn't bring in hardly any money. It was going to be a hard winter for them.

"No." I shook my head. "I can use my Pa's coat."

We went to the back aisle of the store, where anything and everything that a lumberjack could need was sold. Mr. Whiteside was right helpful while I picked out my gear.

When we were about done, Hugh and I stopped up at the front counter. There were some fine-looking knives all set out under the glass, including Bowie knives, hunting knives, and some woodcarving knives. I wasn't there to buy a knife. But you know how it is when you have money in your pocket and you're ready to spend some of it, you look at all sorts of things that you really aren't interested in buying.

There was one knife in particular that caught my eye. I asked Mr. Whiteside, "Can I see that one?"

He reached under the counter, pulled it out and handed it to me. It was a Jim Bowie blasé, about eight inches long and about two inches wide. I ran my forefinger and thumb along the steel of the blade.

Hugh whistled low.

I heard a low chuckle from behind me. "Too much blade for a boy," an accented voice broke in.

Irritated, I glanced around to see a dark-haired man with a lean, tanned face. His hair was longish and tied back. His shaven cheeks were darkly shadowed and he had bright blue eyes that were laughing at me. He was a big fella with arms like ham hocks. His chest was broad and his legs, thick, and he stood with them wide apart. His shirt was a bright and bold red, and he carried himself with confidence. My father would have said that he was a man who was comfortable in his own skin. I knew that I was looking at a real woodsman, a lumberjack.

"I'm headed up north," I remarked. "You can run into all sorts of wild animals in the woods. This here knife might come in handy."

"You gonna gut a black bear with that knife, boy? Or maybe a badger?" He laughed out loud, baring big, white teeth. He had one of those deep laughs that seemed to echo through the cluttered store.

I looked around, worried that other people would hear how he was poking fun at me.

"Hey, Augie, this boy, he is something." The newcomer was a Quebecois, French Canadian. My pa had had several fellas from those parts to supper over the years, so I recognized the accent.

I saw that Mr. Whiteside was chuckling, too.

"You never can be too careful," I mumbled.

Hugh rolled his eyes.

"A black bear is more afraid of you than you are of him," the French Canadian continued. Then, he reached over and, without a by-your-leave, took that blade right out of my hand. "And badgers..." He gave an expressive shrug. "They are fierce. If you are close enough to a badger to touch it with a knife, it had better be dead or in a trap."

"I was looking at that knife."

The laughter went from his face just like that, and he looked at me hard. "Are you buying it?"

"Uh, no. I mean, I don't know."

"Augie, throw the blade in with my other things."

"What I meant was I hadn't decided," I protested. I didn't like this fella coming in and running me over.

"I am doing you a favor," the man responded. "Now you will not cut yourself." He ran a finger across his throat demonstratively. "I will pick it all up in the morning, Augie. You have it ready?"

"Yes, it'll all be ready, Fabien."

"Well then, À bientôt. I have plans for this evening, so do not be expecting me early." He clapped Mr. Whiteside on the back, and, without another glance at me, strode out of the store, whistling.

"Do you know who that was?" Hugh's eyes were wide with admiration.

"Fabien Roget," Whiteside said. "Some say he's the best riverman on the Chippewa."

"Yeah, well maybe I'll be a river rat, too, come spring," I announced, lifting my chin high. That Roget might be bigger and older, but that didn't make him a better man than me.

Augie chuckled, clearly dismissing that possibility.

"Could I see that knife again?" I asked. It was such a fine looking blade, new, without a nick in it. Of course, we'd never had one like it. I would be nice just once to have something shining and new that I didn't really need. I could just see myself as a lumberjack, working the pines, with that trusty knife strapped to my side.

Mr. Whiteside shook his head. "No. You heard him – Mr. Roget's buying this one. If you're interested in a knife, I can show you some others."

I shook my head. "Nah." The truth was I didn't have the money for any knife. In a way, Roget had let me off the hook. I mighta bought it had he not come in. The money that I earned this winter would be going to my family. But, I promised myself, if I had any left over, I would come right back here and buy myself a knife just like Roget's.

Mr. Whiteside began to add up my purchases. "It should be quite a winter for logging. I've heard talk that the lumber companies are gonna try and send a couple-million yards of board feet down the Chippewa this spring. Wouldn't that be something?"

I tried to make my response sound like I was in the know. "I don't know if Half Moon or Dell's Pond can hold that much timber."

"Which outfit will you be working for again, young man?"

"The Daniel Shaw Lumber Company," I said it proudly, well-respected outfit it was. "Just like my Pa."

"Who's your father, boy?" Mr. Whiteside asked.

"Gustav Andersen," I said. "He's one of the best sawyers in these parts."

"Gus Andersen? I heard tell that your father was hurt in an accident at the mill."

"Broke his leg bad. But Doc Foster says he should get better. The leg's set. Now he just has to give it time." I'd heard Ma and Pa talking late at night when they thought we were sleeping. I knew that they were worried Pa's leg might not heal right. If he was lame or worse, he would have a hard time going back to lumberjacking.

"Your pa is a good man." Mr. Whiteside looked like he was about say something else, but Hugh interrupted him.

"Hey Sevy, come take a look at these peaveys." Hugh held up

the tool of the river pigs, who herded the logs harvested in the winter down the rivers in the spring. The long handle was smooth and finished and there was a metal spike and a hook at the end for moving the logs. A picture flashed into my head of me, poised on a thick log using my peavey to break up a log jam in front of an awed audience. River rats were the daring heroes of the lumber industry. They risked life and limb herding the logs through frigid waters and over treacherous rapids. But then the reality that I wasn't sure that I had the money for the peavey as well as the other gear had me putting it back regretfully.

"No sir, I don't need it."

Mr. Whiteside took the peavey and handed it to me. "Take it, young Andersen. It's on the house. A while back, your father did some woodworking for me and gave me a real fair rate. Take the peavey. I hope it brings you some good luck. You Andersens are due for some."

I nodded my head, a little choked up. It sure did seem like us Andersens had been gettin' a raw deal lately.

I paid for the lot, waited while Mr. Whiteside wrapped it up for us, then we headed out.

"Like you need any more luck." Hugh snorted. "No more school. You get to be a lumberjack this winter and Whiteside gave you a peavey." He wielded it in the air, striking the sign for the apothecary's shop we passed by.

"Hey. Watch what you're doing." For a moment, I thought about how my pa's face was pinched with pain and my ma's with worry. That didn't feel too lucky. I shook my head.

"Yup." Hugh gave me a cheeky grin. "Hey, wait. Clancy's Sweets Emporium is down there."

"I want to stop somewhere else first." We continued down the street, past a tailor, a music store, and a grocer's. The day was progressing, and the sawdust covered street was filled with horses and conveyances of all kinds, drays, moving vans, and an ice wagon. One carriage had a particularly fine-looking matched pair of bays.

"Randall Park," Hugh and I said at the same time. A fancy looking team like that had to come from the neighborhood where the wealthy folk lived, the homes of the mill owners and lumber barons.

Even though I was nervous about where I was going, and I had a very specific place in mind, I couldn't help smiling at Hugh, shaking my head. He just didn't let things bother him. He was always along for the ride, no matter where it took us.

We turned a corner, headed a few blocks up a smaller street, and were met with the acrid odor of burning horse hooves. I paused outside of a barn that adjoined a small, white house.

"Oh, I see," Hugh muttered. "You think she's here?"

The street sign read "Jaeger-Farrier." Wrinkling my nose against the stink, I poked my head inside the opened door. The clash of metal on metal erupted from the back of the shop.

"Mr. Jaeger. Mr. Jaeger," I called. But there was no response. Clearly, he couldn't hear me over his work. I took a step in. It was hot and smoky inside, even with the door open.

Mr. Jaeger, a thick set, bald, stocky fellow was shoeing a Percheron. And holding the horse was the very person I'd come to see, a girl with a thick braid of dark blond hair.

"Hel-lo," I called out. Still they didn't hear me.

Using some long clamps, Mr. Jaegar pulled the red hot shoe out of the fire and pressed it onto the horse's hoof. The hoof sizzled. Smoke rose up around them.

16

Hugh picked that moment to try to push past me through the door. Not thinking, I pushed back. Somehow our legs got tangled up. I pulled one way. He jerked the other. Then we were both face down on the ground.

That got the Jaegers' attention. Big Mr. Jaeger turned his head to the side and spit, then eyed us suspiciously. Adelaide Jaegar stared at us. Both Hugh and I scrambled to our feet and I felt the blush creeping up my cheeks. Thankfully, we hadn't spooked the Perchie.

"*Was ist los?*" Jaeger spoke in his native German first, then, seeing who it was, asked, "What do you want?"

I dusted the dirt, hay and straw off my clothes. Then, I picked up my packages, which were, thankfully, wrapped. Hugh still had the peavey, which he had somehow managed not to stab me with when we fell.

"Afternoon, Mr. J-Jaeger," I stuttered. "Adelaide."

She had some soot on her face and a piece of straw in her hair, but when she smiled at me, it was like seeing an angel. Now, ordinarily, I would never have had the nerve to do what I was about to do, but I didn't know when I'd be back in Eau Claire, and I wasn't going to waste this chance.

"You boys are needing something?" Jaeger asked. Mr. Jaegar had a deep voice and a definite accent but he spoke English well, as did his daughter.

"We were just doing some shopping," Hugh explained grandly, like it was something we did every day, "saw the smoke and decided to stop in."

I glared at him and shook my head.

Adelaide rattled something off in German and I only caught the word "*Schule.*" Jaeger grunted and turned back to his work.

Standing there, my arms full of packages, I felt foolish. I hadn't really thought this out. I had just wanted to see her once before I left.

"Let's go." Hugh elbowed me.

"No."

"The candy store." He wiggled his eyebrows expressively.

"In a minute."

He groaned but still I didn't move.

"Well, are you going to talk to her?"

But I wasn't paying any attention to him. My eyes were on Adelaide. Now that her Pa's back was turned and he was bent over with a horse's hoof in his huge hands, she shyly met my glance. My heart pounded.

"I'm leaving Eau Claire. I'm going up to a logging camp near Siren," I said it loud enough so that she could hear me— the most words I'd ever said to her.

She nodded, just looking at me.

"Well, goodbye then."

"*Auf wiedersehen*, Sevy. Goodbye."

There was nothing else to say, so I turned and headed out of that barn, walking tall. *She'd spoken to me.*

"What was that all about?" Hugh demanded once we were outside. "You got a shine in your eye for the blacksmith's daughter?" When I didn't respond, he was quiet for a moment, mulling things over. Then, he went on, "If you like her, then why'd you up and leave like that? You could of talked her up some more. You aren't going to see her again until summer."

He was right. I wouldn't see her again for months. Suddenly,

I didn't feel so smart anymore. But it had taken all my nerve just to walk into that barn and say "hello." I hadn't really thought the whole thing out. Adelaide probably thought I was some kind of fool.

"Come on, Sevy." Hugh took mercy on me by letting it drop. "Let's go get some taffy and a root beer." He took off down the sidewalk.

Feeling kind of downhearted, I followed him.

* * * *

I was busy that night, getting ready to leave early the next morning. Though it was just October, early days for the log camps, there was work to be had for those who were willing to help set up. While packing my bag and doing some final chores, my head was going in ten different directions. Peter and Marta were all worked up, too, so it was hard to get them to go to bed in the little room that we three shared.

I was ready to turn in when Pa said, "Sevy, come sit with your ma and me for a while."

Pa and Ma were sitting by the fire. Ma was doing some mending by the light of an oil lamp. Pa was sitting up in the chair he'd carved.

The two spoke softly to each other in Norwegian, which they did when they didn't want us kids to understand what they were saying. Over the years, Ma had picked up Norwegian from Pa. Peter, Marta, and I knew some Norwegian, but since our folks wanted us to be real Americans they spoke to us almost always in English.

"Sit down, Sevy," Pa directed. "These past few weeks, you've done a man's work for this family."

"Yes sir." Had I packed everything I'd need? Had Adelaide

thought at all about me since I'd seen her that afternoon?

"*Ja*, life is not easy at a logging camp. But for you it will only be for this one winter. Then, you will come back to Eau Claire and go to school," Pa said it like he was trying to convince himself of the truth of his words.

"Yup." I nodded.

Then, he was quiet for a moment. Pa was a proud man and I knew sending me to work in his place was real hard on him. If he could have worked with his busted leg, he would have. I shifted on my seat, my mind, wandering. Maybe I'd write Hugh a letter from the camp. He'd like getting a real letter. "How often does the mail get picked up at camp?"

"*Uff da*, Sevy. This isn't a game. Are you listening to me?"

"Yes, Pa. Sure am."

"Go easy, Gus. The boy has a lot on his mind." Ma looked up from her sewing. Her eyes were bright and teary. She always was one to cry, at sad or happy occasions.

"Sevy, listen close because you'll be on your own from tomorrow on," Pa continued. "You'll have to act like a man even though you're a boy and your life has been soft until now."

"Soft?" I bristled. While he'd been layin' in bed, I'd been bustin' my rump doin' his work and my work, too. "I do chores and you said yourself that I've worked hard since the accident."

"Don't interrupt me," he growled. Pa may have been restricted to his chair but he was still a bear of a man with dark eyes that could pin you down.

I squirmed on the wooden bench.

"Your ma and I have wanted to make things better for you than they were for us. I know this house ain't much, and it ain't our own. But we were getting closer to having our own land. If only this hadn't happened." He gestured to his leg. "I wouldn't let you go north if there were any other way." He looked away from me.

"Pa, I know that." Sure, one day, we'd have a farm of our own. We'd all heard it so many times and the truth was that something always got in the way of us saving the money we needed. One of us kids would get sick or Pa would have to send money back to Norway for his father's funeral. Still, I knew we were better off than a lot of the other folks who lived in Shaw town. We always had enough to eat and a roof over our heads.

"I left Norway when I was just a little older than you are today. Pappa, your grandfather, was a *husmand*, which meant he rented the land he worked and the cottage we lived in. But he could never work hard enough to buy something of his own, and he saw that would never change. So, he told me to leave. He gave me what money he could and then I left Pappa, Mamma, my brother, my sisters, and my country. I worked my way to Hamburg, Germany and from there to New York. I took a steamboat up the Hudson River to Albany, a canal boat to Buffalo, and then a sailing ship to Chicago because I'd heard there was work to be had there. It was in Chicago that I met your mother."

The way Ma was now looking at Pa smoothed away all of the worries and troubles on her face. In the firelight, she looked younger, a lot like Marta.

"I know, Pa. I know. She was working as a seamstress." We kids had heard this story about a hundred times.

"My parents had come to this country together when I was a little girl. My father died right after they arrived in Chicago," Ma said. "Morsa, my mother and your grandmother, was a seamstress, and she made a living for us in Chicago. But she always talked about us having a farm of our own one day. It was what my father had always dreamed of, what brought him to this country. But it wasn't possible when it was only the two of us." Her voice sort of quivered. "Morsa died a year before I met your father."

I didn't want to hear more. I had things to do. Besides I knew all of these old stories and none mattered to the new life starting tomorrow.

"The night before I left, your grandfather, Anders," Pa continued, "called me to him. He said, 'I won't be there to tell you what to do or how to act. But remember to treat everyone else as you would want to be treated, be honest, work hard, and the rest will take care of itself.'"

Fighting to stifle a yawn, I jumped when a big, warm, callused hand clamped down on my arm. "Be a man that other people can count on."

"All right, Pa."

Ma said, "Come here, Sevy. You take good care of yourself. Be careful."

I could tell Ma was near crying. She set her mending down and held out her arms. Now I ain't a little guy any more, but I went right into Ma's arms and I held her tight.

"Sevy, come here." Now it was Pa calling to me

I turned and hesitated for a second, I couldn't remember when Pa and I had last hugged. When I pulled back from him, I could see that his eyes were suspiciously bright as well.

"G'night Pa and Ma," I said, and my voice cracked. But I didn't care. Up to this point, it hadn't seemed real. Leaving school and telling everyone I was going away had been fun. But now I was going to have to pay the fiddler. I was leaving the next morning for a lumber camp far from home and from my family. I'd never even spent single night away from my ma and my brother and sister. Now I was staring down the nose at a winter working in the woods with a bunch of fellas I'd never met.

It was tough falling asleep that night. I was too worked up. And so, I listened to my parents talk until late. I didn't really even pay attention to what they were saying. I just wanted to hear the sounds of their voices.

Chapter Three
~ Heading North ~

Eventually, I must have fallen asleep. But it didn't seem like any time had passed at all before I felt a hand shaking me awake.

"Sevy. Sevy, wake up. It's time," Ma whispered trying not to wake up Peter and Marta. "Mr. Walsh will be coming for you soon. Wash up and get dressed. I'm making some tea."

Slowly, I sat up, leaving my blankets behind. I shivered in the cold air. Ma had a fire going, but it wasn't doing much in the way of warming the place yet. It was pitch black outside. Winter with its short days was definitely coming. I made my way over to the washstand. I braced myself to shove my hands into the ice-cold water. But, to my surprise, I found the water was warm. Ma must have heated it up on the stove for me. But then today was an important day, the day I was to leave Eau Claire, alone, for the first time in my entire life.

The main room was a little warmer than the bedroom.

"I'm brewing the tea right now." Ma worked at the stove. "Your breakfast is almost ready."

I nodded, distracted, thinking about what I might of forgotten to pack.

"Morning, son," said Pa. He was already sitting in his big chair by the table. In the hazy light of the gas lamp, he looked bleary-eyed, like he hadn't slept real well either. His mouth was closed in the thin, tight line that told me he was hurting.

"Pa"

"Sevy, you have everything ready?" Ma asked.

"Yup. My rucksack's right by the door."

"Good," Pa said with a nod. "Dan Walsh will be here come daylight. Isn't that what he said?" Pa looked to Ma.

"Yes, Gus. I told you what Edith Walsh told me. Dan is delivering some tools near Mondovi. He'll bring Sevy that far and then he'll help him find a ride north."

"Good," Pa grunted. "Sevy, you'll be in a Daniel Shaw lumber camp within few days.

Ma placed a thick slab of bread with butter and cheese melted on it in front of me. Next, she gave me a mug of tea so hot that I had to set it down on the table. "Eat your breakfast, Sevy. You don't know when you'll get your next hot meal."

As usual, I was starving. So, even with the two of them sitting there watching me, I devoured all of my breakfast.

Then Pa shoved his plate over to me. "I'm not hungry, Sevy."

I didn't need much convincing and I was licking the butter off my fingers when there was a soft knock at the door. After some hurried hugs and kisses, some hastily whispered words, I was wrapped up in a blanket on a wagon bound out of Eau Claire. It was then that I realized I hadn't said goodbye to my little brother or sister. In all of the excitement, it had plumb slipped my mind.

The next few days passed in a cold, hungry, confused blur. At night, I slept in strange farm houses, eating meals with folks I didn't know. Days I spent cold and, more often than not, wet riding in wagons north, always north. Eventually, about a week after I left Eau Claire, I arrived at the lumber camp that was to be my home for the next few months.

To be honest, the first time I saw that small cluster of buildings, I wasn't real impressed. I'd expected something bigger, grander for the heroes of the Northwoods.

The fella driving the wagon spoke up, "Here we are, boy."

"Yup." I nodded. "Thank you, mister." I couldn't for the life of me remember his name. I'd ridden in so many different wagons with so many different drivers over the past few days.

The clearing was cut right into a white pine forest. The rough hewn buildings were made of logs that had likely been chopped down right here and they were set in a rectangle around the clearing. I didn't see anyone moving around, but that made sense as it was the middle of the afternoon.

We pulled up to the biggest building. Almost immediately, the door swung open and a thick set, red-faced man in an apron stepped out.

"Harold," the driver greeted the other man.

"You have my flour?" he grumbled. "I had some unhappy lumberjacks last night when I didn't have any doorknobs for them at supper."

"Got a couple of bags for you."

"Camp's getting bigger every day. We need to be stocked up for when the snows start to come. These mine?" He reached under the oilskin and patted a burlap bag of flour.

"That whole pile is for you. No, not that one. It's for a Knapp, Stout, and Company camp that's on a forty north of here. And I brung you somethin' else, too. See that youngun over there." He gestured at me with his thumb. "Him, too."

Harold eyeballed me, as if taking my measure. Then, he spoke, "I'm Harold Hildreth, camp cook. Leave your gear on the ground over there and help me get this flour into the cookhouse."

I jumped down from seat and did as I was told. I tossed a fifty pounder of flour over my shoulder and followed Harold into the building. We passed through the lean-to and I saw a chest with a lock on it and a sign that read "Wanigan." Next, we stepped down into the main building. Here, despite the low ceiling, I could stand up straight since the building was set into the ground. Several large wooden tables filled the space and a monster of a stove dominated the room. It was all clean as a whistle and a rich meaty smell came from the cast iron pot set on the stove. A skinny boy with sandy blond hair who looked to be about my age was sitting in one corner peeling potatoes.

"Where do you want 'em?" I asked.

"Just set them right there on the table," Harold said. "What's your name, boy?"

"Sevy. Sevy Andersen."

"I'm the cookee here," the potato peeler announced, glaring at me. "We don't need no other boys. So you can go right back to where you come from."

"I'm not here to be a cookee," I responded. "I'm a lumberjack."

Harold and the potato peeler burst out laughing.

"No. Really. I'm here to be a lumberjack." I stared at him real hard and set my jaw. There was no way anyone was gonna talk me out of a lumberjack's pay. My family needed that money. "Just ask Mr. Lynch. He's the Push, right?"

"Rest assured, I'll be talking to Joe," Harold responded. "But how did you end up here?"

"My pa's Gus Andersen. He worked this outfit last winter."

"Gus is a good man. A hard worker and a heck of a sawyer. I heard that he got hurt bad. How's he doing?"

"Better."

"How's he getting around?"

"Crutches."

Harold eyed me, clearly expecting me to say more. "You're a man of few words, like your Pa. Well, if you're gonna be lumberjacking this winter, we're gonna have to feed you up. Don't ya think, Bart?" Harold chuckled at his own joke because the potato peeler, Bart, was all skin and bones. Harold caught my glance and chuckled. "I'm the best cook in this county. You shoulda seen Bart a month back."

"I'd rather be a cookee than a jack any day," Bart snapped. "I eat good and I'm warmer than those men out in the woods. The cook's probably the most important man in this camp, except'in the Push. And I'm learning to cook. By the time that I leave this camp in the spring, I'll be ready to be a camp cook in my own right."

"Now don't go getting too big for your britches, Bart. You've got a lot to learn yet."

"That's just fine," I agreed, but there wasn't no way I would want to be a cookee. I was here in the Northwoods to draw a man's pay, a full dollar a day, as a lumberjack.

"Well, boy." Harold turned to me. "I can't just stand around here chewing the fat. I gotta get supper ready. This here's the cookhouse, as you can see. You'll eat here twice a day. Bart brings the grub out to where you're working at midday. You passed by the wanigan on your way in. That's where you can get some necessaries you might of forgotten or used up. Now, you'll be needing to meet the Push and Dob O'Dwyer, he's the clerk. Bart, why don't you do the honors."

Bart nodded, set down the potato he was peeling, and wiped his hands on his apron.

"Don't be dawdling, Bart. Those taters will be waiting for you."

Bart tugged off his apron and headed towards me. "Come on."

I followed him back out of the cookshack and into the clearing around which all of the logging camp buildings were arranged. Out in the cold air, I could smell the promise of snow in the air.

"Lemme grab my gear." I scurried over to where I'd tossed it and Bart slouched after me.

"That there's the filer's shack." Bart pointed a thumb over to one of the smaller log buildings. "He's a grouchy codger, but he does a good job keeping the saw blades sharp. But you probably already know all about how a logging camp works, don't ya? Your Pa being a jack and all. Usually, I take church ladies who come to the camp around, give them the tour, and they don't know nothin' about logging camps."

I nodded, though, to be honest, I hadn't known exactly what a filer did. My pa was indeed a man of few words, and when he was with Ma and us kids, more often than not, he let us do the talking.

"That there's the blacksmith shop." Bart gestured with his thumb at another log building right by the filer's shack.

"That big one there is the horse barn. There're two teamsters at this camp and a couple of fine teams of Belgians. I get to drive one of them hay-burners to the woods when the jacks are dinnering out. Cy's his name, the horse I mean, and he's blind in one eye. But the jacks say he has a second sense for when a tree is coming down. This here's the clerk's office."

Bart knocked and a gruff voice called out, "It's open." So, we strolled right in.

"Shut the door. You're letting in the winter with you, boyo." The voice was kindly with an Irish lilt to it.

My eyes slowly adjusted from the brightness of the out-of-doors to the dim lamplight and I saw two men. One wore spectacles, had a kindly face, hair that was near white, though he looked to be about Pa's age, and was seated at a desk on which was set an opened ledger. The other fella who was standin' was tall, thick and broad with a dark head of hair and with a no nonsense air to him.

Dropping my bag, I took my hat off to show respect, the way that my ma had always taught me.

"Mr. Lynch," Bart spoke up. "This fella's come to be a lumberjack."

"My name is Sevy Andersen." I supplied.

Lynch looked at me real hard. He didn't smile and his eyes were cold. "You Gus Andersen's boy?"

I nodded.

"You have the look of him."

I nodded again.

"The boy doesn't have much to say." The Irisher observed.

"Talked just fine in the cookhouse," Bart mumbled.

"Some of these Norwegian fellas can be tight lipped. Why one of the fellas from last winter, I don't think I ever heard five words out of his mouth. Showed up one day with a `Hello,' and then left six months later with a `Goodbye.'" The Irisher commented, as if that explained it.

"I ain't full Norwegian. I'm half really, and there ain't nothin' wrong with that. My Pa's was one of the best sawyers at this camp or at any of the other logging camps around the Chippewa and he's a full blooded Norwegian." My voice cracked on the last words.

"Well, you do talk," the Irishman said with a smile, as he put his pipe back between his yellowed teeth. "I didn't mean any disrespect, Sevy."

Even Lynch was smiling now. But on his face, a smile looked hard, like rock breaking. He nodded to me. "I'm Joe Lynch and you can call me Mr. Lynch or Push. Your father said you can do a man's work in his letter. Is that true?"

"He looks kind of scrawny to me," the Irisher commented with his head tilted as he assessed me. "Tall, but spindly."

I began to panic. What if they didn't give me a chance? What if they decided that I was too young to draw a man's wage? My whole family was relying on me. I had to convince Joe Lynch to let me stay on.

"I may be skinny, but I'm strong. And I'll work hard. Harder than anyone else here. I promise you, Mr. Lynch, you won't regret hiring me."

"That's quite a promise," Lynch commented. "And, I'll hold you to it." He held out his hand to me. "Your father said much the same, and his word's like gold to me. Welcome aboard, Sevy."

I took his hand. His palm was callused and hard and he gripped my hand the way he might hold onto an axe. But I gripped him right back, the way I'd been taught. The way a man would. And even though he squeezed mine real hard, I didn't flinch or try to beat him. Pa had taught me to have a firm grip, but he'd also warned me that a man who tries to win a handshake wants to show you who's the boss. I already knew that Joe Lynch was the boss, and I didn't plan on giving him any grief.

"This trouble-making Irishman," Lynch said once he'd released my hand, "Goes by the name of Dob O'Dwyer. He's our clerk here. You'll get your pay from him come spring."

"Just call me Dob."

Not sure how to take him, I nodded to him resisiting the urge to shake my hand to get the blood back in it. Dob grinned right back at me, showing a big gap between his two front teeth.

"Bart'll take you over to the bunkhouse. You can settle in for a bit and then it'll be supper time... You boys get going, Dob and I have some business to take care of."

Once we were back outside, Bart looked at me. "So that wasn't just talk about you being a jack."

I thought he must be impressed. So, there really wasn't any need to say much more. "Yup."

"That's a relief," Bart shook his head. "I was worried you was gettin' hired to help the teamsters out as a stable boy. That's the job I got my eye on. I really like workin' with them horses. They're smart, ya know. Come on, I'll show you where to stow your gear."

He led the way across the clearing to another long, low log building. "This here's the bunkhouse." He pushed the door wide for me. The first thing that hit me was the smell. Sure, I'd been around hard working men my whole life, but the stench in that dark shack about knocked me over after the fresh out of doors.

"I already stoked up the fire in the stove so it's good and warm in here when the fellas get back. They lay their wet gear there on those rails by the stove to dry them off."

Once my eyes had adjusted, I saw that bunk beds lined both walls and a massive stove dominated the center of the room. Wooden benches were set around the stove and along the interior of the bunk beds.

"Pick any empty bed and stow your gear away. Lots of fellas been comin' in these past few days, so there aren't a lot left. Pick one. I gotta get back to the cookhouse. When you hear the dinner call, come on over."

"Yup and thanks," I said. Then, Bart was out the door and gone.

Alone now, I eyeballed the bunks. There were a few empty places at the back of the bunkhouse. But Pa had warned me about those. When it got real cold in January, the men who slept there would likely feel the wind coming in through chinks in the wall. You could pack them with mud or snow, once it came down, but those were cold spots. And when it came time to sit on the preacher's benches by the stove, those men could get stuck at the back. I didn't want to be up front, but I also didn't want to be cold for most of the winter.

That was when I saw it. There was a top bunk right by the stove and, for some reason, no one had taken it. It didn't make sense. It should have been one of the first to go. But why question good luck? So, I headed over there and threw my gear right up on top.

The straw tick mattress smelled pretty fresh. I laid my bedding out on it and and was stowing away my gear when I heard the Gabriel horn for the first time. It was calling us all to supper. Quickly, I rolled up the rest of my kit, hopped off the bunk, and headed out the door.

By now, it was already beginning to get dark. The air had that fresh cold taste to it that warns that there may be snow coming. I drew my coat closer around me. I made a quick stop at the outhouse and then headed over to the cook shack.

I was one of the first fellas in the door. It was downright hot in there from the stove which was nearly glowing red. Red faced and working hard, Bart was throwing some more logs into it. The place smelled wonderful, like a holiday feast. I saw piles of biscuits, beans, salt pork, potatoes, and some molasses. It was more food than I had ever seen lain out in one place. I was eyeballin' it, figuring out where I was going to sit, when the door burst open. An army of men marched in. They weren't talking. Instead, they just came right on in and took their seats.

I stood there and watched them. Then, realizing that I was starving and going to get left out if I didn't get a move on, I wiggled my way through the crowd and found a place at the far end of a table. Neither of the men on either side of me looked at me. They were just reaching for the food. I was just about to ask for the butter, when I remembered what my father had said to me: "There's no talking in the cookhouse."

"Why?" I'd asked him.

"At a lumbercamp cook shack, there are men from all over the world: Irishmen, Norwegians like us, Frenchmen, and usually some Indians, Chippewas or Lakota. How would it be if all of those men from different places started talking? There'd be arguments and then fights. No Push wants that kind of trouble. So, the rule is no talking allowed. Remember this, Sevy."

Pa had warned me about this more than once, but in those first few seconds, I'd almost forgotten. Thankfully, it came to me before I'd opened my trap. So, I joined the men on either side of me devouring the mountains of food on the table and there sure was plenty to eat.

My ma was a fair cook, but she didn't have a thing on Harold Hildreth. I hadn't eaten since early that morning. I filled my plate a couple of times and I didn't slow down or come up for air until I'd done justice to everything. Then, I paused, looking over at the man sitting to my left. Ma always said it was poor manners to do what he was doing, using his biscuit to mop up the butter, salt, and bacon fat on his plate. But seeing as no one paid him any mind, I did the same. Nothing tastes better than a biscuit doctored up in this way. It was warm, salty, and rich. For dessert, Bart set out trays of apple pies.

Feeling like I was going to pop, I tilted back, leaning my shoulders against the rough log wall and sliding half off the bench. I didn't think I could manage another bite. I just sat there tired and pleasantly stuffed.

I looked at the men in the room. They were just like the men I'd grown up around, the ones who worked at the mill in Shaw town in Eau Claire. They may have come from all different places and looked different. But they all had lived hard, were strong, rough, and none too clean.

Some of the men began to wander out of the cook shack, letting in drafts of cold air that barely managed to keep me awake. I was sleepy. The room was warm and comfortable and my belly was full. My head began to bob.

Someone tapped me on my shoulder, startling me awake.

"Sevy Andersen, right?" A short, brown and gray whiskered man looked down at me. He seemed to be about my father's age. "I'm Christian Walker. The Push says that you're to help me with the icing tonight. The road monkeys have cleared some trails. Feels like it's gonna freeze tonight. So if we could lay down some ice, we'd be that much closer to having those trails ready for when the snows come. Can you be ready in fifteen minutes, out at the barn?"

The idea of heading out into the cold darkness when I was already dead beat wasn't appealing. I'd thought I'd get a good night's sleep in before starting to work, but as my ma always said, beggars couldn't be choosers. "Sure, Mr. Walker."

He nodded briskly and headed out.

I'd come up to the pineries to work as a jack and to pull a jack's wages. But I also knew that the new fellas were often called upon to help out with other jobs. I wasn't one to complain. So, I headed back to the bunkhouse to grab my outdoor gear.

* * * *

Getting the logging roads ready for the logging sleighs was important. After the road monkeys had done their work, teams of horses headed out, pulling a barrel of water on a wagon or a sleigh. The idea was to drip the water over the logging roads to make them hard and slick. Horses could pull much more weight when pulling a sleigh with runners on ice than a cart with wheels in the dirt. That was why logging was done in the winter, so the logs could be moved more easily. Then, in the spring, with the thaw, the logs could be run down the river to the sawmill towns. Of course, I understood all of this. It just seemed a little early to me to be laying ice what with no snow on the ground.

Mr. Walker was out waiting for me, holding onto the reins of a team of gray Perchies. "Sevy, this here's Bob and this is Sammy. Bob's a sweetheart, but Sammy's ornery. Look, see how he pins his ears back at me and curls his nostril."

I swallowed hard. They were enormous beasts with massive, muscular bodies. Sammy lifted a hoof and I glimpsed a massive horse shoe with caulks in it near as long as my finger from my knuckle to my joint.

"So they don't slip," Mr. Walker explained, seeing my eyes on them. "Icy ground can be slippery. Let's get going, Sevy. It's just getting colder out here."

I shivered in my coat and then followed Walker's lead and climbed up into the wagon.

First, we filled up the barrels on the cart over at the creek. Then, we drove over those logging trails until the barrels were empty. My job was to help with the filling up and then to watch off the back of the wagon for when we were out of water.

I can't tell you how many times we went back to the creek. I thought it wasn't ever going to end. My face felt frozen. I could barely feel my hands in the woolen mittens my ma had knitted for me. It seemed like I got wetter and colder each time we filled that wagon. I was sure my hands were frost bit. And I was tired. I'd never felt so dog tired before in my life. When we finally returned to the camp, I could barely keep my eyes open.

Mr. Walker patted me on the shoulder. "Sevy," he said, "You go hit the sack. You did good tonight. I'll take care of the boys."

I nodded, too tired to talk. I didn't bother arguing I would help out with the horses. I was too far gone.

I stumbled as I entered the bunkhouse. After being out in the moonlight, it was near pitch black in that low slung log house. Some men were snoring real loud, the whole place was shaking, and it stunk to high heaven. Once I was inside the door, I shucked off my boots, tucked them under my arm, and walked in the rest of the way on my stocking feet.

"Dang it!" I muttered when I stubbed my toe on a bunk post. I saw a body shift in one of the other bunks. I heard someone pass gas. But none of that bothered me none. I was dead set on getting to my bunk. The top of the stove was glowing dully red, and between that and the warm bodies, the place was almost warm inside. I could just make out my bunk to the left of stove. Real gingerly, aware of the man in the lower bunk, I sorta grabbed the top of the upper bunk and hoisted myself up, dropping down, right on top of a big, sleeping body.

"*Sacré bleu!*"

Next thing I knew, I was on my back on the bunk, pinned with a thick, hairy forearm pressed down into my neck and the tip of a blade pressed to my chin.

"Who are you?" a deep, accented voice demanded.

"I'm Sevy. Sevy Andersen." My voice came out harsh and whispered because of the pressure on my throat. "Please don't kill me, sir."

"Fa, a boy." Just like that, the pressure was gone. The bunk creaked and groaned as my attacker straightened and jumped off of the bunk. He struck a match and lit a lamp. Next, he shoved it into my face. I was blinded for a moment, but then saw a lean, bearded face glaring down at me. He had dark beard and wild hair, dark eyes, and a mean, hungry look to him. Right now, he looked plenty riled.

"Boy, what are you doing? You wake me up again and I'll kill you."

"Hey, keep it down, Roget," someone called out.

"Yeah, we're trying to sleep," another jack grumbled.

Suddenly, I realized I'd seen this man before. Heck, I'd probably even seen the blade he'd been holding to my neck. It was the French Canadian I'd run into at Whiteside's General Store.

"I'm real sorry, sir. I didn't know you were up there. I didn't think this bunk was taken. It was empty earlier and I left my stuff there."

He snorted at me incredulously. "This bunk is mine. A lesson for you, *mon fils*, the best bunk always goes to the top woodsman. I am the best. Me, Fabien Roget."

I wasn't about to tangle with a grizzly bear, so I nodded. "Yes sir. I'll find another place to bed down." But then a thought struck me. "Where's my gear?"

"I threw it outside. It was on my bunk," he said as if that explained it.

"We gotta work tomorrow," one of the men muttered.

"That's enough," another grumbled.

But Roget ignored them. "Go, boy. Don't bother me again." He blew out the lantern and hopped back up into the bunk.

I was left standing in the dark feeling I'd been punched in the stomach. I had to get my gear and find another bunk, but I was frozen by what had just happened. I sure didn't want to wake up some other fella. Near in tears, I swallowed the lump in my throat and started to shuffle away. I might even have an enemy. I just wanted to go to sleep and wake up in my own bed with my ma making me breakfast. And that Frenchman had thrown my gear outside! Now that was just plain mean-spirited.

I headed to the door and back outside. In the moonlight, I could make out that it had begun to snow. Peering around, I saw some darker lumps just to one side of door. I had been so set on getting to bed, I hadn't noticed them before. I reached out slowly, afraid it was a coon or a badger. But it didn't move none, and even though it was a little damp, the blanket that everything was wrapped in felt familiar. I picked up my bundle and hugged it close to my chest. Then, I sorta slumped down there, outside the bunkhouse, with the rough bark of the logs digging into my back.

It began to sink in that I was alone, far from my home and family back in Eau Claire, and I didn't have any friends around me. To tell the truth, I may even have cried a little out there in the snow and the moonlight. I sat there 'til I started to freeze and only then did I go back into the bunkhouse. Moving as quietly as I could, I managed to find a bunk far from the stove and by a drafty wall. I fell right asleep.

Chapter Four
~ Logger ~

The days that followed were a blur of work and bone tiredness. I'd never been so beat or so all out hungry in my entire life. The mornings were getting colder. But we got up while it was still dark outside. We headed out when the Push could see his axe blade in the morning light. One morning, I made the mistake of asking Mr. Lynch what the temperature was. He answered that it "was fine weather for logging." Later, I learned that he would never tell anyone the real temperature. I guess he worried that it might make us balky if we knew just how cold it was.

I started out working days as a road monkey— shoveling manure out of the iced ruts during the day and helping to ice them over at night. This was about the lowest job at the camp. I figured they were testing me, so I didn't dare say anything. But I hadn't come to the Northwoods to work as a road monkey, and I needed to earn a lumberjack's pay. If I stayed a road monkey, I would come away from the season with less than we'd figured.

I steered clear of Roget, though I did ask Bart about him one night while he was cleaning up after supper.

He raised an eyebrow at me as he lowered a pile of plates into the wash basin.

"He's French Canadian."

"And?"

"What are you two boys gabbing about?" Harold asked, one thick eyebrow cocked. He was a chatty fellow when the cooking was done.

"Sevy's asking after Roget."

Harold mopped at his sweating and reddened face with a rag. "Roget's a legend in these Northwoods. Heck of a jack, a first rate top loader, and probably one of the best river rats on the Chippewa. He's been working for the Daniel Shaw Company for going on five years. If you want to learn about how to be a lumberjack, Sevy, he's the man to learn from."

True as that may be, Roget seemed to have taken a disliking to me ever since that first night in the bunkhouse. He didn't speak to me and barely acknowledged me. I doubted he would be teaching me much of anything.

Lumberjacks worked six days out of seven. Then, thank the Lord, after a week of working harder than I could ever have imagined, on Sunday morning, the Gabriel didn't ring and there was no call of daylight in the swamp. I woke up at the usual time, but when I looked around and didn't see anyone else stirring, I pulled my blankets right up to my neck, curled up on my side, and closed my eyes. If the Lord could rest one day, so could lumberjacks.

I didn't wake up until nearly midday. I slept until the grumbling of my stomach got me up and dressed. Then I headed on over to the cook shack and ate my fill of doorknobs, bacon, and beans. After I'd washed the meal down with some black lead, I felt like a new man. Then, I headed back outside. I ran into Bart who was carrying an armful of his togs.

"Whatcha doin', Bart?" I woulda thought he would still be working to clean up the after the meal.

He scowled at me, his face darn near as red as his hair. "Cook makes me wash my gear every Sunday. Once, he even made me take a bath! I told him it could be the death of me, but he don't care none. He says if I ain't clean and smellin' like a rose, than I ain't got no place in his cookhouse."

My pa had told me that Sunday was the day for doing wash and writing letters at a lumber camp, and I had slept away half the day. So, I hurried back to the bunkhouse, grabbed my gear and headed over to the washhouse. I'd helped my ma wash clothes, so I knew what I was doing. But still the job was cold and wet and took some time. I passed on taking a bath, myself. Afterall, bathing too often, especially in winter, can make you sick. Besides, greybacks like clean bodies better than the ripe ones. At least, that was what the old timers said.

After hanging up my wet gear by the stove in the bunkhouse, I headed back outside. There, a group of jacks had gathered in the clearing in the middle of the camp and about twenty feet away from them stood a target. I'd noticed it before, but never seen anyone use it. It was just an eighteen inch wide log stuck into the ground standing about five feet tall and with a red bull's eye painted on it. Other larger rings surrounded the bull's eye, each a little further out.

"Hey there," I said to no one in particular.

"Shh." One of the jacks shushed me as a couple of other fellas frowned at me.

"What?" I whispered back.

"Watch."

All eyes were on Roget, who stood a little off by himself. He eyed the target, holding onto that axe like it was an extension of his arm. He swung it smoothly back in an arc behind his head. Then, in one smooth motion, he swung his arm forward and released the axe straight at the target. There was a swoosh and then a thump as the blade went right into the target. I saw that the blade buried deep in the bull's eye. Someone whistled and few men applauded. It was a heck of throw and near impossible to top.

The Push took Roget's place. He swung his axe more forcefully than Roget had readying for his throw. His action was more about power than grace. His axe flew just as true and landed in the log, a hair to one side of Roget's. Both in the bull's eye.

Now the other men cheered and commented, but I could feel the tension building. Neither of these men was used to losing.

Dob, who stood off to one side of the crowd leaning up against a hitching post, said, "You know, Fabien, some men wouldn't call it good sense to try and show up the boss, even in a game."

Roget laughed, baring white teeth against his black beard. "You think I should let him win?"

"I'm just saying." Dob drew deeply on his pipe.

"Ah, *la vie est courte*," Roget shrugged. "Life is short. What is there to be afraid of? That I take the long walk? To another camp down the road? No, I think I am not so easy to replace."

"I ain't lost yet," the Push interrupted, not angry, just focused. "Don't be so cocksure of yourself. Let's take it out another ten feet, boys."

One of the jacks walked off the distance and dropped a branch down on the ground to mark the distance. Two fellas rolled that stump over to the spot and then set it upright. Now I'd seen axe throwing contests in Eau Claire, and these were usually decided by twenty feet. I knew that I was seeing something special when those two fellas stepped up to a mark on the ground a full thirty feet away from the target. Again, Roget stepped up to throw first. Once more, he swung his arm back, his eyes narrowing on the target. He didn't hesitate. Releasing his axe, it flew straight and true directly into the bull's eye.

A few of the fellas applauded. The Push stepped up next. He eyed that stump, squinted at it, squared up his shoulders more than once. Then, he swung his arm back, but just when he should have released, he caught himself, adjusted his feet, took a deep breath, and got ready to throw again.

In the excitement, I think I forgot to breathe. Suddenly, I realized that I didn't want Mr. Lynch to win. He was my boss and he was giving me a chance and all, but I wanted Roget to win, because he was the real deal, a lumberjack through and through.

Mr. Lynch muttered to himself, adjusted, swung again and released his axe. Somersaulting through the air, it flew at the log. But this time it plunged into the log a little below the bull's eye.

Roget had won. Men cheered and clapped and everyone congratulated him. I caught a few of the jacks looking at him enviously. The Push didn't seem too upset about the outcome. He'd lost fair and square to the best woodsmen in our camp and probably in most of the other camps along the Chippewa.

Now, up until this moment, life in the logging camp had not been at all the way that I'd hoped it'd be. But looking at Roget, I had a new sense of excitement. He was the sort of man I hoped to become one day, brave, fearless, skilled, and respected. Sure, I looked up to my pa. He was a good man, but he wasn't showy. A typical Norwegian, he thought a man should never "talk himself up." But Roget had flare. He made bold statements, and he backed them up with actions. He was exactly the sort of man I wanted to be. I took a deep breath and walked though that crowd of lumberjacks right up to him. "Mr. Roget, I'd be real appreciative if you could teach me to throw an axe like that."

He stared at me for a long moment, saying nothing.

Dob spoke up. "This here is Gus Andersen's boy, Sevy."

Roget looked right at me and an odd look crossed his face, like he was seeing something downright unpleasant. "This is not a game for children." He adjusted his toque, turned, and walked away from me without another word. I stood there staring after him, confused.

"Did you see that?" Bart grabbed my arm. "That Roget's some jack."

I didn't say a thing.

After that, a few of the other fellas stepped up to throw axes. But with the real action was over, the rest of the fellas wandered off. There was still plenty of time before dinner. Some took naps. Others played cards. I wrote a letter home. It was tough to do 'cause I didn't want to sound whiny, but all I could think about was wanting to be home. I mean I knew I had to stick the winter out, but having time to think about being home, well, it made my stomach hurt.

That night, being that it was a Sunday, we had a fine supper. Then, some of the men pushed the tables to the sides of the room. A fella named Billy Whitacre took out his fiddle and played some tunes. Another jack on a squeezebox joined him. Then, fellas were up and dancing.

I wasn't gonna dance. My belly was full and the room was warm from the fire and the bodies, leaving me half asleep. So, I closed my eyes and daydreamed that I was at a real dance, a Christmas one. Instead of fellas stompin' around, there were ladies all done in up in pretty dresses and I was standing around with Hugh, the way fellas do. The fiddlers were playing a lively tune and then Adelaide came in. She looked right at me and she smiled. I smiled back. Then, feeling bold, I walked right across that dance floor. I nodded to her friends, but kept my eyes on her. I couldn't get over how pretty she was in her blue dress with her blond hair braided up in a crown, the way those German girls do. Then I was standing in front of her, I reached out for her hand and...

A cloth landed on my face startling me from my daydream.

"Sevy, here, you wear the apron. I'm done dancing." Bart's voice pulled me back to the present. He collapsed on the bench beside me as I sat up. He was breathin' hard.

"What?" I asked, confused and all out of sorts. I pulled the cloth off my face, held it up, looking at the apron.

"You be a girl now. I'm done dancing.

"No. I ain't pretending to be a girl." I didn't want any part of it, even though the fellas looked like they were having a good time. I wanted to be back in my dream, in Eau Claire with Adelaide.

I headed out of the cookshack and back to the bunkhouse. I opened the door and found Dob O'Dwyer sitting in the amen corner with a group of men gathered around him. Dob was doing the talking, as usual. Wanting to be alone, I nearly groaned aloud. For a moment, I hesitated until Dob eyeballed me, one caterpillar-thick, white eyebrow arching over a blue eye.

"I'm just headed for my cootie cage," I explained unnecessarily. I gestured at my bunk. He nodded, tapping his pipe on his hand.

I headed over to my own bunk, pulled off my boots and hung up my coat and socks to dry out. Laying down, I tried to get comfortable, smacking at a greyback that bit into my thigh.

"You all know most of my stories," Dob protested. "I don't have any new ones to tell."

Jerry Smith, a young swamper who was in his second year in the Northwoods protested, "I ain't heard 'em all yet. Please Mr. O'Dwyer, tell us one."

"Well, perhaps I can think of something. What kind of story do you want? Maybe a legend of these Northwoods? A Paul Bunyan tale or something about his grand ox, Babe?

Dob didn't take much convincing, I thought as lay down staring up at the roof. He was a born storyteller, the sort who would like to never shut up.

"A true story," another jack ventured.

There was a moment of silence, then Dob continued, "There is one story that I haven't told before and, to the best of my knowledge, it's true. I heard it from a man at a camp north of Hayward a few years back. He swore that what I'm about to tell you is the God's own truth.

"There are mysteries in these northwoods. They're old, ancient. The Indians tell that animals and spirits made these woods home long before us white folks came in.

"I want you boys to think about how it feels to walk through the woods on a moonlit night. The way the snow reflects and the shadows dance in the moonlight. Think about walking into a virgin growth of pine, how the trees whisper to each other. These

Northwoods are alive, and I feel it most of all by some of the lakes. At sunset, you sit on the shore and look out over the water and see a sturgeon leap out of the stillness, cleaning the sand out of its gills, and you feel the power all around you."

Enchanted by his words, I propped myself up on my elbow and peered down at him. I'd felt echoes of what Dob was describing, but I sure wasn't going to say so in front of the other fellas. So, I waited and listened.

"Now, boys, I've stood on the black rocks of Lake Superior and I've seen the white-tipped waves crashing on the shore. I've watched bald eagles soar and heard the cry of the loon at twilight. I tell you, this Northland is special, and if I were a religious man, I would say blessed."

I looked around and saw all of the men were listening hard. They were men who lived close to nature and each understood the mystery and the majesty that Dob was describing.

"The Ojibwe Indians were here before us, but before them, another Indian tribe lived up in these lands. I don't know who they were, and I don't expect many can tell you. But they built huge mounds in the ground in the shapes of animals... Have any of you ever seen anything like that?"

"There were some near Rice Lake," one of the men offered. "I used to visit a girl up there, but she went and married a farmer. I saw a couple of them shapes."

"Now, I've travelled a good many places in my near fifty years," Dob continued, "and I can tell honestly that you feel something in a place like that. You feel it down in your bones. Like it's sacred. Do you know what I mean, boys?"

There were a few grunts of assent.

"Well, according to the fellow who told me this story, there was a land speculator and a lone wolf, one of those fellas who scout out trees to harvest. These two had teamed up. The land speculator sent the lone wolf out to some forties of prime timber up near Ashland.

"The lone wolf found some good parcels and planned on claiming them for the speculator as soon as he got to a government office. But then he heard about some real fine stands of trees by some Indian lands. These lands hadn't been touched yet because the Indians believed that the land they were on was sacred.

"Still, the lone wolf headed out to check the land for himself. What he found was an untouched forest of giant white pine. The land was flat and the trees so huge that the ground was near bare under them. And it was quiet amongst those trees, like a living soul hadn't been to those parts in a long time, even the birds were quiet. All he could hear was the sound of the wind whistling through the trees. In the center of these woods was a clearing, and there that lone wolf found the mounds. He walked around them one at a time. He recognized the first one as a white tail deer. The second one was bigger and he had to climb up a tree to make out the shape. Once he had a bird's eye view, he saw it was a bear. He walked around for some time, but felt mighty peculiar, like someone or something was there with him the whole time, watching him. He recognized that he was somewhere special and felt like he was intruding, that he shouldn't be there at all. So, he climbed back down, left those woods, and walked back to town."

A couple of the men muttered and grumbled at this.

"Now." Dob held up his hand. "I know that it sounds unlikely that a lumberjack would just walk away from some prime timber. But you all know that lone wolves can be an odd group. Too much time alone in the woods sometimes makes them peculiar. All I know is that this particular lone wolf felt there was something not right up in the forest near those Indian mounds, that it was a place that should be left alone. When he met with his boss, the speculator, the lone wolf told him about the other forties he'd scouted, so that the speculator could file the claims. But he held off on mentioning the forest near the mounds. He just didn't feel it should be bothered.

"But, later that night, he ended up at a watering hole with some other fellas. They had a few drinks and started playing some cards. As the evening wore on, the lone wolf got to talking and he told the story of the mounds and the great pines surrounding them.

"Well, work got back to the speculator, who was a sharp fella. First thing the next morning, he registered for those lands and that fall he sent a lumberjack crew to work those forties. This is where the story gets strange. For, you see, bad luck plagued the crews. The first group set up camp. But even before the first snows began to fall, they all got sick. They never got well enough to work that winter, and they cleared out before Christmas. The speculator sent up a small crew the next winter. Now, I didn't believe this when I first heard it, but the fella who told me this story swore it was true, none of those fellas ever went home. No one knows what happened to those men. Their camp was cleared out of all their gear. They just vanished. None of their families ever heard a thing."

Someone snorted.

"You can doubt all you want, but this is the story that I was told. The third winter that speculator had just about had it. All of his other lands were producing. There was money to be made from those pines by the mounds and he decided that he was going to keep a close eye on things. To make sure that the job got done, he personally visited that camp. One night, he was sleeping in the bunkhouse on a top bunk near the door, in a spot not unlike where young Sevy is sleeping. In the dead of the night, he heard a scratching at the door. He ignored it. A few minutes later, he felt something cold and wet touching his hand. He thought that there was snow blowing in through the cracks, so he tucked his hands under his blanket. Then, he felt that same cold touch on his feet. He thought some dog was licking or sniffing at them. This got his attention. He sat bolt up right, ready to tear into the fool dog that was keeping him up, but rather than a dog, he found himself staring right into the red eyes of the biggest black bear that he'd ever seen."

Dob growled low and deep, a sound that sent shivers down my back.

"That bear dragged the speculator right off his bunk and out of the cabin and into the woods before any of the fellas in that bunkhouse could do anything about it. Even though they were spooked, that crew searched the woods for their boss that night and the next, but there wasn't a sign of him, not even a scrap of clothing. It spooked them all something fierce. A few days later, those men lit out and never returned. Story travelled the camps, you know how they do, that those forties were haunted and I believe that to this day, those pines still stand."

For a few minutes after Dob finished telling his story, the other men were silent, digesting the words.

"Tell us another one," one of the jacks asked.

"Come on, Mr. O'Dwyer," Jerry Smith begged.

"No, I'm done for tonight, boys. We all have to get some shut eye. We gotta work tomorrow."

There were a few more complaints, but most of the fellas took the next few minutes to settle in for the night.

When the lamp was shut off, I lay flat on my back up in my

bunk, staring up at the roof, and thinking about that bear and the speculator. Even though I knew Dob's story was nonsense, I made sure to tuck my feet and hands more securely under the blanket, not that a blanket was going to stop a bear. Still, I fell right asleep.

I woke up in the middle of the night because I had to take a piss. I slipped on my boots and a blanket over my shoulders and headed outside. I'd unbuttoned and was peeing when I heard a growling, low and deep, behind me. Half awake, I knew it was the bear coming to get me. I turned to run, tripped over the laces of my undone boots, and fell face down, ass up into a snow drift.

The snow was miserably cold, but not as miserable as I felt when a group of jacks stood over me laughing down at me. They were still laughing as I pulled myself out of the snow, shivering and wet. I didn't even bother changing my wet long johns when I climbed back into bed. I just pulled my blankets over my head, hunkered down and tried to ignore the chuckles and the ribbing.

"Boy better watch out for that bear."

"I don't know if I'd go to sleep, Sevy. That bear may come for you again."

"Did you see the look on his face?"

If I could have died of shame right then and there, I would have.

Chapter Five
~ Bad Decision ~

I was still working as a road monkey when the Push put out the word that I was to learn how to be a real barkeater. So the fellas started teaching me. Even though I think I got in the way more often than not, I was starting to feel like a woodsman. I could remove a brush with a grub hoe, work a cross cut saw, and fell a tree as well as anyone. I was earning my keep.

I should of felt better, and I did mostly. But the nights were still tough, especially those nights when I pulled double duty and helped Mr. Walker ice log roads. On the trails at night, the loneliness would sink into my stomach 'til I could barely breathe or swallow. It was worse then, because I had time to think. Time to feel sorry for myself. I often wondered how Pa could do it year after year, the being alone part, I meant. Sure, at camp there were fellas all around you, but they weren't your kin. And Pa had left us each year for as long as I could remember to go to the Northwoods. Then again, I knew what drove Pa. He'd told me himself many times. It was that fool dream he had of having a

farm of his own. He wanted it so bad for all of us that he could taste it. And only now, when I was so far from home, living with strangers and working like a dog, could I really understand the price of that dream, because now I was paying it.

On the night I wish I could forget or at least do over, Mr. Walker wasn't doing too well either. He was sick, coughing nonstop and with a runny nose. After an hour or so of icing, I could see that he was barely able to stay upright in his seat. The problem was, with the temperature well below freezing, it was prime icing weather.

I yawned and, taking off a mitten, rubbed at my eyes. I was plumb worn out myself.

"Sevy," Mr. Walked said. "I just ain't up for more tonight. I'm likely burning up with fever. Could you finish the last few trails alone? And then tend to Bob and Sammy?"

Bob and Sammy, Walker's Perchies, were his livelihood and his family. As a hay pounder, or horse teamster, his livelihood depended on them. So I knew that it meant something that he was entrusting them to me. But I was so tired I could barely see straight. Still, I answered, "Yes sir, Mr. Walker. I'll take care of the boys. I'll finish up those last few trails."

Mr. Walker smiled weakly. "Thanks, boy. And don't forget to scatter hay on the downslopes. Tomorrow morning, you sleep in. I'll explain to the Push."

Numbly, I nodded. I drove the team back to the camp and dropped Mr. Walker off at the bunkhouse. Then, I continued on with icing the logging trails. Being out there alone, in the darkness, with only Bob and Sammy for company, it was different, scarier. It was likely there were all sorts of wild animals around, wolves, badgers, and maybe even an angry bear roused from his winter's sleep. Still, I worked diligently. It was near the middle of the night when I finished icing all of the trails. There were a few smaller log trails where I hadn't spread any straw on the downslopes, but I figured I'd done more than my share for a fella working alone. In the morning, I'd tell Mr. Walker about those trails.

Back at camp, I tended to Bob and Sammy, just as I'd promised Mr. Walker I would.

Chapter Six
~ The Accident ~

The next morning, I ignored the call of "Daylight in the Swamp." It felt like heaven to pull the blankets up to my ears while all the other men were trooping out. I slept until near dinner time when Bart was sent in to wake me up. Once I was geared up, I joined him on the wide, flat seat of the sled which was loaded up with hot food for the jacks who were dinnering out since they worked a forty far from the camp. Bart clucked to the old gelding, Cy, and we were on our way.

For the first time in a long time, I felt good. It was a beautiful, bright, winter day. Sunlight glanced off of the snow and ice sickles hung from some of the bigger trees. Christmas was fast approaching, so Bart had put sleigh bells on the rig. They tinkled cheerfully with our gentle movement down the trails.

It may sound peculiar, but I felt like singing again. Things were finally beginning to work out for me. I was managing to do my job and help my family out. Pa and Ma would be proud of me. For a few minutes, my world was fine.

Bart turned old, swaybacked Cy down a narrow logging trail where the ground was a little sloped. We were in the thick of the woods where hundred-foot-tall pine reached for the sky. There wasn't much but snow on the ground between the trees. It was shady and cold amongst the giant trees, which blocked out the warming sunlight. The trail dipped slightly and just beyond it, I could see Mr. Walker's flea bitten pair, Bob and Sammy, hitched up to a load that a crew was piling high with logs. Another teamster worked a pair of logging horses to cross-haul logs up the skid poles and onto the load using a single chain. They were working on a third row of logs and the bottom two rows of logs had already been secured with the chain wrappers. Fabien Roget worked as the top loader, using his peavey to adjust the logs as they came up.

It all happened right before my eyes. First thing, the sled they were loading sorta eased a little sideways. I saw Sammy shift a little and then Bob snorted. I watched Fabien raise his arms up, as if balancing himself. Next, I heard the scraping of the runners slipping on the iced trail, a trail that had no straw on it.

Mr. Walker shouted as the sled began a sideways slide down the slope. "Haw!" he yelled at his team. "Haw, boys! Haw!"

"Holy smokes!" I watched in horror as it appeared that whole log-filled load was about to spill right over. A couple of fellas jumped out of the way. The other team of horses jumped around.

"Haw! Get on boys!"

Urged on by Mr. Walker, Bob and Sammy fought the shifting weight of the sled.

In the commotion, I'd lost sight of Roget. But now, I saw him. Somehow, he'd gotten down off the load and around in front of that slowly slipping sled. He stood there where that whole load could come right down on him. With his peavey, he hooked a log from that third row, tugged it down, and thrust one end down onto the frozen ground. Then, he tugged a few more down, bracing the load. With the weight lightened and those logs bracing against the sideways slide, the sled stopped. It was canted sideways and Bob and Sammy were off the trail hip deep in snow and jittery, but all right. Mr. Walker spoke softly, calming them down.

"*Merde!*" Exploded into the silence. "*Merde!*" Roget continued on in French, gesturing with his hands at the ground, shouting at everyone and no one in particular."*Paille*," he said. "Where is the straw?"

"There's no straw on this hill," Walker observed.

Cy chose that moment to toss his head, and bells tinkled merrily through the woods. Roget, Walker, and all of the other men on that crew looked right over at me.

That's when it hit me and my heart sank into the giant gaping hole that opened in my stomach. This was one of the small logging trails that I hadn't gotten around to putting straw on the night before, and I hadn't remembered to warn Mr. Walker that morning.

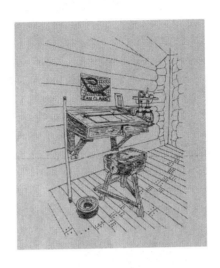

Chapter Seven
~ Punishment ~

The Push sent for me after supper. He was waiting for me at Dob O'Dwyer's office. Roget and Mr. Lynch were there, too. I had never been so scared in my life. Was I gonna get fired? Was Mr. Lynch gonna wup me for putting his team in danger? Or was Roget gonna kill me and get the whole business done with?

Mr. Daly spoke first, "Sevy, there could have been a serious accident today."

I nodded.

"Men and horses could have been hurt or killed because you weren't responsible. You understand that, boy?"

I nodded again, swallowing the enormous lump in my throat. I bit the inside of my cheek to keep from crying. I noticed I was looking down at the floor. I made myself look up again 'cause my Pa always said to look a man in the eye, even when you've done wrong.

"I... I'm real sorry, Mr. Lynch. I meant to tell Mr. Walker that I didn't get straw on those last couple trails. I was so tired."

Moving like greased lightning, Roget grabbed me by the front of my shirt. "You think that being sorry is enough?" He let go of me and I fell back. He waved his hands about, real worked up. "You think now that everything is all right? I told you before, Joe, this is no place for a school boy."

"Let's be clear, Fabien, no one got hurt," the Push stated.

Roget spat on the floor in disgust. "The Northwoods is no place for a boy." Shaking his head, he went over to the mantle and leaned up against it, staring down into the flames.

"Sevy," Dob spoke up calmly from his seat behind the desk. "An accident was avoided, but barely. On a logging team, each man has to rely on the others to do their jobs. If someone doesn't, well, then a fellow can get hurt. Or worse."

"It was so late and I was..." I shut my trap when I saw the Push raise his hand.

"I'm not interested in excuses," he said. "Excuses don't do anyone any good when a man gets hurt or killed because of a mistake. Sorry don't feed his family."

"No excuses," I repeated softly. I set my jaw and nodded my head. All three men were staring at me and I knew that what I said next really mattered, so I thought for a minute. "You're right. I don't have any excuses. I made a mistake, plain and simple. But it won't happen again. I mean I can't promise I won't ever make a mistake again. But I can tell you I won't make this one. I'm learning more each day. I..." My voice trailed off as I watched an unspoken communication pass between Dob and the Push

"The problem ain't that you didn't get all the trails iced, you know, boy," Mr. Walker said. "I wouldna gotten 'em all done myself. But you gotta let the other men on your team know the score, so no one gets hurt."

"Yes sir."

"Send this boy home to his mama," Roget said. "He will be glad for it. I hear him crying into his pillow a night."

A blush of shame rose in my cheeks. Roget had to be lying, I assured myself. I wasn't ever loud enough that the other fellas could hear me, was I?

I looked at each of them in turn, but there was no softening of their expressions. Logging was a serious business. For a few seconds, no one said a thing and I figured that I was a goner.

Finally, Dob spoke. "Gentlemen, it seems a bit extreme to me to fire Sevy over a mistake which didn't have any consequences," he observed as he drew on his pipe. "We are all too worked up about something that just didn't happen."

"An ounce of prevention is worth a pound of cure." Mr. Walker offered me an apologetic glance. "My horses could have been hurt."

"Still, there was no real resulting loss. I do the books here," Dob continued. "In real money, the boy cost the company a half day's work from Fabien, Christian, and the other members of their team. I'm talking about the time it took to straighten up the mess. The way that I see it is that the most fair way of handling the entire situation is to dock Sevy's pay to make up for the lost work. I think we should give him another chance, Mike." Dob was on my side, though I didn't know why or how.

The Push and I eyeballed each other. I didn't let myself look down though I shook in my boots.

Mr. Lynch looked away first. He exhaled slowly, running his

fingers through his hair. "You understand, Sevy, that being part of a logging team means being responsible for every other man, no matter if you are sick or tired or both. You got that?"

Hardly daring to breathe, I nodded. "I do. I understand."

"You mean to keep this schoolboy then?" Roget demanded, disbelief thickening his accent.

"This isn't up to you, Fabien," Dob responded.

"Nor to you, old man." Fabien sneered. "You aren't in the woods with this child."

"No, it ain't up to either of you," Mr. Lynch said. "This is my job. Settle yourself, Fabien. All right, Sevy. We'll dock your pay. But one more mistake and you're on the first supply sled out of here. You hear me? We can't afford no more."

"Thank you, sir. I won't let you down." I exhaled in relief. I wasn't gonna get fired.

"You are all fools," Roget snarled. "I will not work with a child. Put me on another team, boss, or I quit."

"Fabien, I won't tolerate any man threatening me." The two men squared off, like they was gonna fight. I'd seen other fellas my own age do the same before tusselin', but it was different when the fellas were big and thick with muscle. "You'll work where I tell you to work. And no more fool talk about quitting."

"He is a boy. He has no place here. Send him home to his mama."

"That's enough, Roget." The Push's tone was ominous, but Roget was too worked up to care.

"You keep this boy or keep Roget, the best lumberjack in the Northwoods." Roget shoved a thumb into his chest.

"Don't talk like a fool, Roget. You know no one will pay you what you get at this here camp."

Roget spun on his heel and stomped out, muttering in French. On the way out, he slammed the door.

Dob calmly adjusted his spectacles.

"I don't mean to make him quit," I said, knowing there really was no choice between an experienced woodsman and a wet-behind-the-ears boy. "I'm not ready to take the long walk, but I won't make another mistake like that one. I've learned."

The Push held up his hand. "Fabien won't quit. That Frenchman threatens quitting at least twice every season... Still, it'd be a good idea to switch you to another team."

"Since Grant broke his arm, those Swedish boys have been short handed," Dob offered. "They won't care who you send them."

I ignored the insult, too scared and desperate to stay on.

The Push nodded. "That's what we'll do then. Take care of it, Dob. I'll go talk to that bull-headed Frenchman." Then, the Push headed out, too. I was left alone with Dob.

He peered at me through his spectacles, one bushy eyebrow cocked. "Don't let me down, Sevy."

"I won't, Mr. O'Dwyer. I promise you, I won't. And thanks."

"Roget doesn't like you and the Push is going to be keeping an eagle eye on you. You have your fate in your own hands. Don't make another mistake. Do you understand me?"

"Yes sir." I headed out of that shack feeling relieved and worried as all get out. I wanted desperately to talk with someone about what had happened, but I wouldn't. I was too embarrassed. I decided I wouldn't even write about it in my letters home.

White Pine

Excuses and apologies weren't worth the paper they were written on. If I got fired, we would have to go through our savings to pay for just livin'. The money Pa'd saved up to buy us a farm gone once again. It was all up to me. I felt like I carried the weight of the world on my two shoulders.

Chapter Eight
~ Frost Bit ~

After the "incident," the days flew past in a blur of working, eating, and sleeping. Determined to prove my worth, I worked harder than I ever had in my life. The crew I was with was headed up by two Swedish brothers, Olaf and Johannes Jensson. Big, blond, burly fellas, they went by Ole and Johan. They didn't say a whole lot, but they also didn't give me any grief. They were just glad to have an extra pair of hands out in the woods.

Christmas came and went and wasn't like any other Christmas I'd known. I didn't even realize it was Christmas Eve until midway through the morning. We got to head in early that day and we had Christmas Day off. But I would have preferred to have worked as usual. Sitting around camp, I felt like the loneliest person in the whole world. Mr. Walker and Dob invited me to play cards with them back at the bunkhouse, but I didn't have the heart for it. I missed my ma and pa, and Marta and Peter. I missed Christmas treats and presents. I missed all of it; I was homesick, real homesick. And for once I wasn't the only one. There were some other sorrowful-looking jacks wandering the camp, thinking about their kinfolk who were far away. Harold put together a special dinner for us, but it all tasted like sawdust to me.

Thankfully, the next day was back to business as usual. That morning, I was one of the first up. I hopped out of my bunk, put on my gear, and headed over to the stove where a pair of my Canadian greys was hanging from a rail. I pulled on those thick wool socks that were nice and warm. Then, I grabbed my boots.

I shoved one foot in and felt my foot slide a little. I wiggled my foot around, then felt a warm, wet liquid penetrate my sock. I pulled my foot out, touched the sticky mess on my sock, sniffed it, and then tasted it. Syrup.

"Dog-gone-it." Someone had poured syrup into my boots.

While other fellas were heading over to the cookshack, I was trying to clean out my boots. My socks were soaked, so I peeled that pair off. I grabbed my other pair of wool socks from where they were hanging. But they were still wet from the day before, and I sure didn't want to put wet socks on. It was cold outside, well below zero.

By then, I was one of the last fellas in the bunkhouse. I heard the door slam. I looked up.

Roget.

I paused, self conscious that I wasn't quite ready yet. He eyeballed me and sniffed. Some part of me deep inside still wanted to impress him, to show him I deserved to be out in the Northwoods, a lumberjack, just like he was.

That was what decided me. He wasn't out the door before I stuck my bare feet into my still sticky boots, pulled on my coat, stuffed my mittens into my pockets, and pulled my toque down on my head. Heading out, I grabbed some grub on the way by the cookshack, and then joined the other lumberjacks on their way out.

It was a good logging day. It was cold but the sun was shining bright and reflecting off the snow. I worked with Aaron Hawkins. He was a patient man who had sons of his own that were just a little younger than me. Working methodically, and talking to me all the while, he taught me the job of barker. Now, it came to me easy enough. I didn't have to think real hard, and the day flew by, and I knew I was one day closer to going home.

Johan and Ole worked their crosscut saw as a team. Now, I watched Roget and his partner, Adam, a fella who was half Chippewa Indian, work. Those two were regarded as the best at our camp. They were artists who did their work with flamboyance, grace, and a complete lack of fear. More often than not, they preferred to go after a tree in the old way, with a single bit axe. They stopped and argued frequently. Still, they were usually the best producers for our camp. These Swedish brothers had an entirely different style of logging. They didn't say much and they weren't interested in doing anything fancy. They simply wanted to cut down as many trees as fast as possible. They could place a tree as it came down as well as any fella, but they didn't care to show off by having it do anything fancy like drive a stake into the ground. Still, the Johnsens worked brutally hard and cut down an enormous number of pines. Hawkins and I had a tough time keeping up.

First, the brothers took turns using an axe to chop a gouge into the side of a tree. The point of this gouge was so that the tree fell in a certain direction. Then, they tirelessly dragged their enormous cross cut saw back and forth across the opposite side of the tree.

Once a tree was down, then Hawkins and I got to work making the log smooth, so it would drag more easily in the snow. We chopped away all of the branches and the bark. Then, the teamsters snaked the logs to the logging road where they were picked up by a sled.

That morning, Johan and Ole were really flying.

When Hawkins paused to catch his breath, he commented, "Those boys never slow down." He grinned as he wiped at his face with a wadded red handkerchief. "Those two are like to wear me out."

"They're not going to wear me out," I commented then spit in the snow. I started to take my coat off.

"Keep that on, Sevy. It might still get colder today, 'specially if the wind whips up. Don't want that sweat freezin' on you."

For a moment, I thought about my sockless feet. Even though my body was good and hot, I could feel the cold seeping into my syrup-wet boots. But I wasn't gonna let that worry me. I was just going to keep working, and eventually they would warm.

That morning fairly flew by we were working so fast and hard. Lunch was hurried and quiet as we were all near starving. We gave all of our attention to our grub. I was near done with my beans, biscuit, and salt pork when I noticed that it was kinda hard to move my toes. My right ones were worse than my left, but I kept wiggling them hard. They were stiff and felt like they had pins and needles sticking into them. I thought about riding back to camp with Bart and tending to my feet when Johan stood up, setting his plate back down on the wagon.

"Back to work," he directed.

About an hour later, I knew something was wrong with my feet. I stomped on the ground, trying to get the blood pumping. I'd heard stories about jacks loosing limbs because of frostbite. I should of taken someone else's woolies. But now that all the fellas were ready to work, I didn't dare say a thing. Anyway, there'd be just a few more hours until dark.

We worked hard all that afternoon. As usual, I was dog tired before the sun went down, and in January the sun goes down pretty early. There was good news, though. My feet had stopped hurting and feeling cold. They felt kinda wooden, but not painful anymore.

We made it back to camp just before supper. So, I didn't take off my boots until I was sitting on the preacher's bench getting ready to hit the hay. A bunch of other fellas in the bunkhouse were already bedding down for the night. I took a seat on the preacher's bench to get a good look at my feet, which had been feeling mighty peculiar all through dinner. I pulled off my right boot. Then, I eyed my foot. It looked kind of whitish, like the blood had been drained from it, and the skin was strange, too, sort of like wet paper. It was ice cold to the touch.

I was still eyeballing it when Dob O'Dwyer spoke up, "Sevy, you been frostbit."

I heard a low whistle. Mr. Walker came up, staring right at my foot.

"How do they feel?" Dob asked.

"They don't really hurt. But they feel sorta strange. Kinda tingly."

"Sevy, that there's frostbite," Walker stated flatly.

Dob sat down beside me and picked up my left foot. He looked it over. "You have to get these taken care of, Sevy."

His words struck fear in my heart. "I don't want to lose a toe." My voice cracked and quivered on my words.

"Sevy," he directed. "Take off your other boot."

I did as I was told and pulled off the other clodhopper. This

70

foot felt strange, too, but didn't look quite as bad. It was more pink than white and I had more feeling in it.

"Those feet need doctorin'," Mr. Walker agreed. "You may need to see a sawbones. You bought some tickets for Doc Jones, didn't you?"

I bit my lip. I hadn't bought the tickets. On the job, lumberjacks often got hurt. It was a risky business. So, they generally bought tickets for care from local docs. Back in Eau Claire, after my pa broke his leg in the sawmill, he used those tickets to get his leg set. But I hadn't wanted to spend money on myself. I'd wanted to save as much as I could. I'd been fooling myself, thinking I wouldn't get hurt. But now I was out of luck. I was hurt and had no money or tickets to pay a sawbones. I shook my head "no."

The bunkhouse door swung open and Fabien Roget came in. He took in the three of us, all standing around somber-faced.

I dropped my eyes, not wanting to meet his gaze. I'd messed up again and I didn't want to hear what this man, who didn't think much of me, had to say about it.

"What's the problem?" he asked.

"Boy's frostbit bad, and he didn't buy no tickets for doctoring," Mr. Walker said.

"I don't want to lose my toes." The words burst out of me. I hadn't cried in front of those men yet, no matter how tired I was, no matter how cold I was, but I didn't want to lose no body parts. It was just too much.

Dob finally spoke up. "I've seen some jacks use pure white lead to treat frost bite. We have some on hand at the wanigan. You smear it all over the affected body part, then cover it first with cotton then a woolen sock. You keep that onto until the skin heals or… " He didn't finish the thought.

"You mean, 'or my toes fall off,' don't cha?" There was a lump in my throat as big as an apple. I wiped at my eyes, which were definitely moist. It just wasn't fair. Heck, I was just a kid. Things like that shouldn't happen to kids.

Roget came over to my bunk. He'd picked up a kerosene lamp on the way. My jaw musta dropped open 'cause I slammed it shut when he kneeled down low and picked up my bare foot in his roughened hands. He turned it this way and that, examining it. He looked up at me as he set it carefully down. "On the river in the spring, I have seen river rats get the frostbite. Here." He gestured at my right foot. "It is just starting. No need for the lead. Warm the feet slowly with water. There is no need for a doctor. I will show you."

And, he did. This French Canadian frontiersman who'd made it clear from day one that he wanted nothing to do with me started looking after me like I was kin. First thing, he cleared it with the Push for me to stay in bed for a couple of days, so that my feet could heal. He made sure that my pay wasn't to be docked during that time. And, true to his word, he taught me how to tend my frostbit feet.

I didn't know what to make of Fabien Roget. He didn't make sense. I asked Dob about Roget again, and he mysteriously said, "You remind him of someone."

"Who?" I asked.

"That's not for me to tell you, Sevy. Fabien will tell you if and when he is ready."

I never did find out who put the maple syrup in my boot that day, but I didn't take it personal. I knew it was just a joke that had gone wrong. Besides, it had all turned out just fine in the end. Somehow, getting frostbit had finally made me one of them, a true Northwoodsman.

Chapter Nine
~ Redemption ~

I stayed in bed for several days and around camp for the rest of that week. My feet felt much better and all my toes stayed where they belonged. Sure enough, I felt ready to go back to work, but Roget and Dob had the Push convinced that my feet needed a few more days to heal.

The Push told me, "This isn't the time in the logging season when you want to lose good men. Get better, Sevy. There's still plenty of days left in this logging season. "

On a bright Monday morning after my week of rest, I joined the rest of the men in the cookhouse. I was geared up and ready to go and I had two pairs of socks on to protect my feet. I was just setting into some steaming oatmeal when the Push clapped me on the shoulder.

"Sevy, you're back sawyerin' on Roget's team."

I near choked on my oatmeal and Bart, who must have come up behind me, pounded me on the back. Red faced, I looked up to see that Roget was right behind the Push. Roget gave me a nod before heading out into the early morning darkness.

"You're back with Roget," Bart whispered as he grabbed some dirty dishes off of the table in front of me.

"I know. I know."

The Push spoke to Hawkins and the Swedish brothers, so

there were no hard feelings. Those fellas were fine with it. After all, Roget's crew had been working short-handed.

Still, my stomach was all twisted up in knots as we headed out to the forty that Roget's team was working. It was on a hillside and the huge pines were packed in tight. It was a tricky spot. The slope made the going hard. You had to be real careful where you put your feet.

Still, the morning went smoothly. It felt good to me to be back out in the woods. I was pleased as could be when Bob Johnson, one of the fellas working the cross cut saw, called me over.

"Sevy, you want to give this a try?"

I nodded eagerly.

He rotated his shoulder around and then nodded to Roget. "Roget said you can spell me. This here shoulder's been giving me some trouble."

So, every hour or so, I would take his place on the saw. Adam Clark, a Chippewa Indian, tirelessly worked on the other side.

It happened when we were working trees on one side of a crevasse. Roget had notched a huge tree. Adam and I had set to it with the crosscut saw while Roget wandered off a few steps behind me, eyeballing the next tree. I was sawing away, but something didn't feel right. I'd only been at this for a few hours but it, the tree, felt wrong. Sure, that saw was going in easy, like it was cutting through something soft and wet. I froze.

"Shoot," Adam broke in. "Why'd you stop, kid?"

"This tree's rotten." But it was too late. There was a cracking sound like thunder as the trunk splintered and began to split in two. And it wasn't falling in the direction that Roget had intended. The big part of that tree was leaning towards where I stood.

They call 'em 'widowmakers' - but it just didn't seem fair that one of them should have my name on it. After all, I was only fourteen years old. I'd never even had a steady girl. But there it was, twice as wide as me, a blur of pine needles and brown prickly branches, blocking out the blue sky. I wasn't supposed to die like this. What were the other jacks gonna tell my ma?

Then, I saw that Roget was right in its path, too.

"Watch out!" I yelled.

There was another groaning creak and Roget turned, his eyes wide.

I didn't think. I saw that tree trunk hanging there, moving inch by inch as the trunk split wide open. And the next moment, I was in motion. There was another unholy crack and glancing up, I saw the brown trunk, a flash of the green boughs. I flew through the air. My body hit Roget's. Then, everything went black.

At first, I thought that I was dead. But something prickly poked my face and something sticky dripped onto my lips.

"Sevy... Sevy? Where are you?" I heard someone calling my name all scared and worried-like.

"Hear anything?" someone demanded.

I heard 'em, but it all sounded strange and far off.

"Sevy!"

I licked my lips and realized that I was tasting pine needles. "I'm here." It came out a whisper. I tried again, "I'm here."

Shards of daylight pierced my darkness. I understood that branches were being pulled off of me. Then, I glimpsed the gray sky and then saw frantic blue eyes and a black beard.

"*Vivant! Dieu merci! Merci, Alain.*"

Roget and the rest of the crew worked to pull me out from under the pine tree. Amazingly, no one had been seriously hurt, though my head didn't feel quite right. When I was free, Roget gave me a hand to pull me up. Then, he bear hugged me and kissed both of my cheeks.

"This boy," he announced, speaking to the rest of the crew, "he saved my life. This, Fabien Roget will never forget."

The other men nodded and commented. I held my head high

despite the tell tale red creepin' up my neck. But after that, we all returned to work as if nothing had happened. That's how it was when you were a jack: one moment, you were eyeballing death and the next, back to work. 'Course, the fellas didn't let me do much of anything for the rest of that day, and I didn't argue much because I felt a little sick to the stomach and tender at that spot on my head. By the time we got back to camp, I figured the whole thing would be old news, nothing special, just another day in the Northwoods.

It turned out, I was dead wrong. It wasn't nothing for Roget. That night, some caterwauling outside the bunkhouse woke me. Some fool was singing loud, like one of those fellas coming home from one of the taverns near our house in Shawtown.

"*Alouette, gentille Alouette. Alouette, je te plumerai.*" The bunkhouse door swung wide like it had been kicked in.

"Hush now, Fabien. The other fellas are already asleep," Dob muttered.

I looked up from my pillow and saw the two of them in the doorway, Roget and O'Dwyer, black shadows against the white brightness of the moonlight on the snow outside.

"Shh. *Ouais.*"

The pair stomped their way in. Then, I heard a thump, like someone bumped into a bunk.

"Keep it down, fellas," one of the jacks said.

"It's Roget," another fella stated.

"*Alouette*" Roget sang out, crashing into another bunk.

"Sure is, and he's drunk as a skunk."

"Some people are trying to sleep here."

"Yeah, keep it down!"

There was more thumping about and muttering. But none of the fellas dared say anything more. After all, Roget was the best knife thrower of the group and no one wanted to mess with him when he was pie-eyed drunk.

What's gotten into Roget? It was sorta like seeing your pa drunk for the first time. I don't know why I did it, and it may have been because I was no more than half awake, but I got up off my bunk, and carefully climbed down, so I didn't kick the jack in the bunk below mine. Then, wincing against the cold floor under my socks, made my way over by the preacher's bench, where Dob had managed to prop up Roget.

"Can I help?"

Dob cocked one bushy white eyebrow at me. He was out of breath and rumpled. He used one shaky hand to press back his forelock. "Yes you can, Sevy. Let's get him on that bunk over there."

Easier said than done, for Roget was dead weight. I took the top half and Dob took the bottom half as we tried to lift the nearly out-cold Quebecois.

He weighed a ton. He turned his head and groaned when I shifted his weight.

"Phew," I nearly gagged when I caught a whiff of his breath. His eyes were unfocused.

We managed to shove him up onto the bunk.

"Sevy, you get his boots," Dob directed.

I had one boot unlaced and was working on the other, when Roget came to.

"This boy. *Oui*, this boy." Sitting up, he grabbed me with one huge hand and dragged me up beside him. "This one is saving my life."

"Yes, Fabien. Sevy's a fine young man," Dob remarked calmly.

Then, to my amazement, Fabien's blue eyes grew moist. "*Mon petit frère.* My brother Pierre, this one." He tousled my hair. "He is like him. Brave. So young. Too young. *Trop petit.*" Roget began to sob, great heaving sobs that shook his body.

"Good Lord, we're trying to get some shut eye," someone

muttered.

"It's Roget." Someone else snorted. "You know how he gets."

Dob pushed Roget back down onto the bunk. Roget didn't protest. In fact, he just kept muttering to himself in French; it sounded like a prayer.

A few minutes later, he seemed to settle. Dob turned to me and said, "He'll be all right now. He'll sleep this off and probably won't remember much tomorrow."

"Do you think the Push'll fire him?" That was the usual consequence for drinking at the logging camp.

"He doesn't need to know about this and none of these fellas will tell him... Poor Fabien. You'll learn this, Sevy, sometimes a man is so filled with pain that he does foolish things to forget about it for a little while."

"I've seen other fellas drunk like him before."

"Some fellas drink for pleasure and some for pain. Regardless, they all end up facing their problems the next morning anyway. I'm not saying it's right, but Fabien, he's got a lot of pain inside him and sometimes it all just spills out. Maybe once a season, he's like this. Tomorrow, he'll be back to work as usual and all of this will be forgotten. I ain't saying it's right, but we all have weaknesses and sometimes it's our Christian duty to forgive and forget. You understand me, Sevy?"

"Yes sir."

"You saved Fabien's life today when you pushed him out of the way of that widowmaker."

"Anyone would have done it," I mumbled, but Dob shook his head.

"That isn't so. You put yourself in danger for him and that's tough for a man like Roget to take. He's pretty much alone in this world. But that wasn't always the case. You see, Fabien had a younger brother, Pierre. When their mother passed on, Fabien paid some folks to take care of the boy. That was the way things were for a couple of years, but Pierre was always after Fabien to let him go lumberjacking with him over the winter. Finally, when Pierre was about your age, Fabien gave in. Those two boys were close and they didn't like being apart."

Dob paused and took a deep breath. "One winter, they were working at a logging camp up near Hayward. There was some kind of accident. I don't know exactly what happened, but I knew Fabien before they went into the woods that winter and I met up with him again when he came out after losing Pierre. He wasn't the same man. Sure, he's still a heck of a lumberjack, but he takes risks that he wouldn't have before. He isn't always careful when he should be, not that he ever puts anyone else at risk. I think he doesn't think he has anything else important to lose.

"I know that Roget's been hard on you. That's probably why he wasn't keen on having you here this winter. Because you remind him of Pierre."

Dob stood up slowly, his knees creaking as he got to his feet. "I'm getting old." He grasped a blanket and tossed it over Roget who was snoring softly. "Go to sleep, Sevy. The morning's coming fast."

I climbed back up into my own bunk with a whole lot to think about.

Chapter Ten
~ A Decision ~

The next morning, Fabien was up at dawn with the rest of us. He looked rough, but he put in a full day's work. He was his usual gruff self with me, but something had changed between us. Maybe it was something as simple as I looked at him different. Before, I'd thought he didn't have a weakness, now I knew better. The difference was that Roget was a normal fella to me now, not a legend like that there Paul Bunyan they tell stories about. Before, I'd thought that Fabien took risks and ran headfirst into danger because he was brave. Now I knew that he took risks because he'd lost everything that really mattered to him.

Days turned into weeks and though it was still so cold that it hurt to breathe and it made my teeth ache, I no longer bothered to ask the Push for the temperature. The truth was I had finally settled in. The news from home was good, too. Ma wrote me a fair amount and from her letters I learned that Pa was getting around a little better each day and that they were getting by. All in all, I was feeling pretty good.

One Sunday night, me and a couple other fellas were sitting on the Preacher's bench just jawin'.

"Just a few more weeks, fellas," Mr. Walker commented with a sigh as he leaned his wiry body back up against a bedpost. "Then, I get to take Bob and Gus home and see my wife and kids."

"There's a pretty girl I know in Chippewa Falls," another fella commented. "I may go get her a store bought hat. Something fine with flowers and ribbons on it."

"If you have a hankering for a girl, don't waste your money on a bonnet," Bob Johnson commented with a leer. Then he grunted as Johan Johnsen elbowed him hard.

"That's enough, Bob," Dob commented. "Some of us here have respect for ladies. Why my Martha, God rest her soul, would turn over in her grave to hear you talking like that in front of these two youngsters." He gestured at me and Bart.

"What are you going to do with your money, Dob?" Adam Clark asked.

"Try to hold onto it past that first weekend." Dob shook a finger at them teasingly. "Each year, I warn you boys to hold onto some of your season's pay. But I can't think of anyone who listens."

"Hold onto it for what?" Ole scoffed. He pointed his thumb at his chest. "I come back next winter and earn more."

"We're saving up." The words burst out of me.

All of the fellas turned to stare.

"I mean, my folks and me. We're saving up to buy a farm of our own."

Ole burst out laughing. "What fer?

A couple of other fellas chuckled and I felt my cheeks flush red.

"Oh, Sevy. It ain't you," Dob responded. "It's just that most of the fellas aren't saving up for something particular. Most go into town their first weekend off and blow a season's pay in just a few days."

I looked at the faces around me and most were nodding.

Bob Johnson asked, "Why save the money? We'll earn more next year."

Johan, who was a man of few words, agreed, "This is what we do. We are lumberjacks."

"Wouldn't want no other life," Mr. Walker agreed, "Come winter, up in the Northwoods is where I want to be."

This comment was supported by a chorus of "Ayes" and "Yups, and a few "Don't ya knows."

"My pa's always talked about us having our own place one day," I said. "We've been saving up for it."

"It's not that we doubt you, lad," Dob continued. "Farming is just fine for some folks. But once you've had a taste of this life, often it's hard to settle back into the harness and work the land. Up here in the Northwoods, a man is truly alive. Some fellas, they just can't give that up."

Johan, Ole, Adam, Mr. Walker, and the others nodded, murmuring in agreement.

I didn't say anything else. What could I say? I found the lumberjacking life tolerable, but I couldn't see myself missing it when I left it.

Caroline Akervik

* * * *

Winter don't gently fade into spring up in the Northwoods of Wisconsin. I thought that particular winter was never gonna end. The cold got right down into my bones and I felt tired and sick. And then, one day when I was comin' in for supper, I saw that it wasn't quite so dark outside, that the days were just a bit longer.

But Old Man Winter didn't let go that easy. Just when I got to feeling better, thinking that I might be warm again sometime soon, we got a heck of a snowstorm that buried us for a few more weeks.

At the logging camp, life went on as usual. But things felt different, maybe it was just in the attitudes of the men. The end was in site. We were all working hard, maybe even harder than before because the Push wanted us to bring in as many board feet as possible before the end of the season. But the men were already dreaming of downtime and of all of the possibilities in the sawdust cities for a man with money to spend.

Some of the men started heading out. As the weeks passed, more and more left camp. It was then that I got another letter from my ma. It read:

Dear Sevy,

How are you? We all miss you and can't wait to see you, in just a few weeks. Your father is doing well. He's up and around with only a little limp. He's been doing some carpentry, and that's brought in some money, but he's fit to be tied with wanting to come up and get you.

I paused in my reading. I didn't want my pa to come get me, not now. It was not that I didn't want to see him. I missed him something fierce. But I wanted to finish out the season. After all, I'd made it this far. Ma ended the letter with the comment:

When you get home, we'll go and talk with Mr. Watters about getting you back into school.

It felt odd thinking about going back to school. I'd grown up a lot over the winter. Grown men had treated me like a man. And they'd expected me to behave like a man, too. Sometimes their very lives had depended me. The idea of going back to being just a boy in Eau Claire felt down right peculiar.

It was Ma's letter and thinking about going back that decided me. The spring log drive was coming up, and I'd been listening to the other fellas talk about it for weeks. They spoke of the adventures of the river rats and about what it was like to ride into town with the logs. This might have been my only chance to be a part of a river drive, and I wasn't going to miss it. It seemed like the most fitting end to my time in the Northwoods. To be honest, I also kept thinking about how Adelaide would look at me when she saw me coming down the Chippewa River on a log raft with my peavey in hand, a real Northwoods hero like from a penny novel.

So I sent a letter back to my folks telling them that I would be a few more weeks and that I was going on the river drive. I knew it might worry Ma. Each year, fellas died on it. But I thought Pa would understand that I wanted to see it through to the end.

Chapter Eleven
~ River Drive ~

All through the winter, we'd stacked huge piles of wood along the banks of the rivers that led into the Chippewa. Now that they were running high, the river rats would push the logs into the mix to be carried downstream to Eau Claire.

I'd heard from the other fellas that the trip would likely take us a little more than a week from where we were to Eau Claire. In the final leg of the journey, flumes would carry the logs down into the holding area in Half Moon Bay. Ever since I was little boy, I'd watched the logs come through the flumes every spring.

When I signed on as a river rat, I traded in my clodhoppers for a pair of caulked boots with sharp points on the soles. I got me some overalls from the wannigan and I cut 'em off half way up my calves. River rats did that so the cuffs of their pants wouldn't get caught between two logs and pull them down under the water where they could drown.

I'd already headed out with the other river rats when they closed the camp down for the year. I was glad not to be there when the last of the fellas pulled out, leaving a camp that had seen so much living all cold, empty, and dead. Before we left, I said my goodbyes to the fellas I wasn't likely to see again. Then, I joined a crew of men including Roget, Adam, and the Swedish brothers. Bart and Harold were coming along to man the cookshack during the drive.

"The grub won't be like the stuff you get at camp 'cuz we're always moving," Bart warned me. "It'll be mostly beans and soggy door knobs."

"Oh you'll be right grateful for any kind of hot food," Harold remarked.

I soon learned neither were blowing smoke.

When I hefted my peavey for my first day of river work, it was with considerable thought. It seemed so long ago that I'd first held it in the general store with Hugh. I cringed to think how green and foolish I must have seemed.

In the early days of the log drive, I learned being a river rat was nowhere near as romantic as I'd imagined. Sure, it was exciting, but exciting in a "you may be killed in the next second" sort of way. Being a river rat meant being cold and wet and worried all of the time, and when you weren't worried, you were all out scared. It was near impossible to put into words the sound of thousands of log feet hitting water that was running high and white.

Several crews worked the drive that spring for the Daniel Shaw Lumber company. The first crew set off early. They moved with the logs, but at the front, making sure that the way was clear for the main body. The second and biggest crew went with the logs, and a third picked up stragglers.

I travelled with the second group. And, of course, Roget was our leader. He was a good lumberjack, but as a rat, he was beyond compare. He had a real sense for how those logs moved in the current. He could see a problem coming up in the bend of a river and knew how to avoid it most of the time. Dangerous work as driving logs down a river was, Roget had a reputation for getting his men through it alive. Even the Johan and Ole didn't give him any guff.

I was wet, tired, cold, but alive. Every step I took on those shifting logs could lead to death. And somehow, knowing that made me feel more alive than I ever had before.

When we got near a town, the folks rushed out to see us and they waved and clapped their hands, though we couldn't hear them over the roaring and grinding of thousands of log feet riding the river.

We'd been on the log drive for a couple of days when the Swedish brothers taught me how to burl. We were in a backwater, pushing out a bunch of logs that had gotten hung up. It was a crisp, cold sunny day, just hinting at the warmer weather coming.

Johan got up on one of the logs first. "Eh, look at me." He balanced carefully on a log and toed it out into the little bay, away from the other logs. It was a real thick log, an easy eighteen inches. He sorta shimmied down the log, standing sideways with his arms up for balancing. Then, he began to walk on the log, making it turn, like I'd seen the burlers on Half Moon do.

"*Snabbare!* Faster!" Ole yelled.

Johan grinned and his feet in their hobnailed boots began to move faster. The log was gaining momentum, turning faster and faster still. Johan's arms were outstretched, his arms bouncing rhythmically with his movement.

"*Bra jobbat!*" Ole said, laughing out loud. "Good job. Keep going."

Johan's legs flew. Then, his torso began to rock, forward, then backward. Then, splash! He was gone. He came up laughing and choking, and splashed an armful of ice-cold snowmelt up at his brother, who leaped backwards.

"You think you can do better?" Johan challenged once he was back on dry land. Arms crossed, he shivered something fierce.

"I know I can," Ole responded, not at all deterred by thought of being cold and wet in the frigid air. Still, he carefully took his coat off and set it on the ground. After some more joshing and horseplay, he got up on a log. But despite his brave words, he didn't last much longer than his brother had.

"Sevy, it's your turn," a dripping wet Johan said after both Swedish brothers had been in and out of the drink a number of times. Both were shaking near uncontrollably.

"Nah," I said.

Johan smacked Ole on the back of the head. "He's no fool. Now the two of us are going to have to go and get some dry clothes."

"Yah, well he can't be working alone now, can he? He'll be heading on back anyway. He might as well get in on the fun."

I was sore tempted. Just like any other kid growing up in a sawdust city like Eau Claire, I'd dreamed of being one of those champion burlers who won the prizes on Half Moon Lake. But I knew that water was real cold, so cold it made your heart feel like it was going to jump right out of your chest. I'd gone ankle deep in it enough times to know. The two Swedes had blue lips, and I'd seen those two fellas jump into snow banks in their all togethers.

"Come on, boy. A little bath won't hurt ya."

"Get rid of some of them bluebacks, so the girls back home will think you're a pretty fella."

They kept at me, and it didn't take much convincing to get me up on a log. Not when secretly I'd been hankering to give it a try.

This was definitely the time and the place. There was no one around but Ole and Johan. And, typical Scandihoovians, those two weren't the sort to tell tales. Maybe a few slow moving musky or northerns might witness me falling into the drink, but even the beavers were still in their dams.

Careful, real careful, with my heart pounding, I stepped from the snarl of logs that had gotten stuck by the shore out onto the log that the Swedish brothers had waded waist deep into the water and held for me. Now, if this here had been a real burlin' contest, I would have had to get up on the log from a straddle in the middle of some log holding pen. But since this was my first time, those fellas were helpin' me all they could. And I didn't want to get anywhere near that cold water until I had to. I guessed I'd end up in it soon enough.

I stepped onto the log, and, keeping my knees bent, I sorta half stood half squatted up. To my surprise, the standing part was pretty easy, the calks in my boot soles dug me right in.

"Good boy," Johan said as he gently directed the log away from the snarl and out into the open water.

I was too busy staring down at that log to say anything back. Then, those fellas, who were at each end of the log, began to turn it, real slow like. I sorta walked with the motion to stay upright.

I was doing it! I was burling!

"This ain't that bad," I shouted.

"Keep your knees bent," Ole instructed.

"Now go faster," Johan yelled.

They began to roll that log so that I had to sorta jog to stay up. The caulks in my boots were now proving more of a hindrance than a help as the way that they dug into the pine slowed down my feet.

"Faster," Johan yelled again.

"No!" But my feet were flying. To tell the truth, I loved it. I laughed out loud. It felt like I was dancin' up there on that log. The next minute, one caulked book sorta got stuck and I took a funny half step. The sky rushed down to the water, and I was in the drink. Ice cold! So cold, it stole your breath away. My heart exploded right out of my chest.

"Holy smokes!" It was only waist deep, but I went scrambling right out onto the shore.

"Good 'un, Sevy." Johan raised a fist in the air.

After that, the icy coldness of the water didn't stop me from getting back up and trying again and again. Finally, none of us could take the cold anymore, so we headed out to rejoin the others at the main drive. But I couldn't stop thinkin' about the burling. I planned on practicing my burling each and every remaining day of the river drive.

The cook shack was tied up on a narrow wooded peninsula. The other fellas sat around a campfire eating their grub when we came up. The three of us were soaking wet, near blue with cold, but also smiling and laughing. Roget took one look at us, didn't saying nothing, just shook his head. We changed our clothes and joined the others around the campfire. I got as close as I could, and even set my boots on some cinders.

While we were wolfing down the beans and salt pork, Johan started jabbering. "This boy," he said, between mouthfuls of chow, "he is a natural on the logs. Give you a run for your money, Fabien. He has young legs."

"Ja, and he doesn't give up." Ole reached over and tousled my hair.

Roget grunted. "No wonder it took you three so long to bring those logs in."

"Tomorrow," Johan said. "You come with us and see him, Frenchman. He is a fine burler, a real river man."

I puffed up at his words, but Roget deflated me real quick. First, he eyeballed me with those cold blue eyes that didn't show a thing of what he was thinking. He stood, tossed the remains of his tea on the ground, then said, "This boy, he is not one of us."

Then, he just walked away.

I stared after him, feeling like I'd been gut punched.

No one said anything for a long moment.

I swallowed my mouthful of beans. I knew there was nothing that I could ever do to prove myself to the man.

Then, Dob spoke, "Sevy, don't mind him."

I nodded, biting the inside of my bottom lip so they wouldn't see my reaction. I wouldn't tear up now, not in front of these fellas, not like some little girl whose feelings had been hurt.

Whiteside spoke up next. "Roget's an odd one."

"What is his problem with the boy?" Johan demanded.

"The problem isn't with Sevy at all," Dob explained. "It's with Fabien. But what he said wasn't right. You're as much of a lumberjack and a river rat as any of us, Sevy, and you've proven it again and again."

The others nodded and grunted and said the things that shoulda made me feel better, but they didn't quite ease the sting of Roget's comment. I thought that he'd come around where I was concerned. Guess I'd been wrong.

Chapter Twelve
~ Logjam ~

The very next day of that river drive, the one thing that river rats fear the most happened. A logjam. For most of the morning, me and the Swedes had been travelling behind the others again, picking up straggler logs. But by midafternoon, we were all back together at the jam. It was a huge one; logs must have been backing up there for days. Fellas from some of the other companies were crawling all over it like ants. There was cursing in many languages up and down both sides of the river. But those logs weren't budging.

Folks were talking and pointing and all fired up about the unholy mess. Through the crowd, I spotted Dob.

"Hey, Dob!" It didn't look like he'd heard me, so I pushed my way through the crowd and grabbed his arm. "What do we do now?"

He cocked an eyebrow at me. "Damned if I know. These fools..." He waved an arm. "Are arguing about the key log."

I knew what the key log was. Anyone who grew up in a sawdust city did. It was the log that held up the whole mess of a log jam. Some folks would tell you that you needed to move a mountain of logs to break up a jam. But others sweared that if you somehow managed to move or pull out the key log, the whole structure would come apart in a swirl of white water and logs.

I was too green to know what to believe. But I stared wide eyed as a couple of jacks climbed over that groaning mountain of wood, following the directions of the Pushes, looking for that one rumored log.

"The only other choice they have is dynamite," Dob said, "but that's expensive for the logging companies — it blows some fine pine to matchsticks — and dangerous for the men handling it." He shook his head. "Find yourself a dry spot to hunker down. We won't be going anywhere for some time."

Some other fella came over and started jabbering at Dob, so he nodded to me and headed on his way.

I wandered around until I found several of the jacks from our company, including Bob Johnson and the Swedish brothers. We got ourselves some cold grub and settled down to watch the show.

From midmorning until afternoon, the river rats from a number of outfits worked with their peavies to break up the logjam. The tension grew, the language grew ripe, and the river bosses grew ever more anxious. More logs just kept coming down and joining the pile up. No one was having any luck. Finally, the Pushes got together and made the decision to finally use dynamite. They would blow that logjam right out of the river by placing dynamite at some critical points at the front of the jam. Now, most of the fuses could be lit safely from the shore, so the fella doing the lighting could get away. But one pack, probably the most important one, was to be set dead center and low down on the pile in the middle of the river. I didn't envy that man his job.

A call went out asking for volunteers. They were looking for experienced men, fellas who would have done this sorta thing before. The problem was that most of the men were savvy as to what they were up against. The man lighting that last fuse was likely to get himself killed. Arguments blew up all around. Each crew had top men, but only a handful would consider taking this monster on. In the end, the bosses chose the jacks they had the most confidence in, fearless ones, men who weren't afraid to die.

I wasn't a surprise the man they chose from our company was Fabien Roget. The crowd parted as he moved through it, walking tall like a knight in those old stories about King Arthur that Mr. Watters used to read to us in the schoolhouse. Roget went right over to the riverbank, unbuttoned his shirt and handed it off. He draped a rope harness over his chest, and then barefoot, wearing nothing more than his cut off trousers, eyeballed that jam.

I knew that he'd taken on a job that was likely to get him killed. But I had to admit that I felt a little jealous as I stood there with the rest of the men watching him. We all knew that we were watching the bravest one of us all, or the most reckless.

"They'll swing his rope over that branch," Dob explained, pointing at a thick oak branch that extended out over the river, "then they'll lower him right down to the middle of the jam, just over the water level. He'll light that fuse then they'll lift him out of there. Hopefully."

Johan whistled low and that sort of said it for all of us. Now I was good and mad at Roget for what he'd said to me the night before, but while I watched as they lowered that crazy French Canadian onto the jam, I felt proud knowing he was one of ours.

Roget was grinning, his teeth, white, against the black of his beard. He was a man living life on the razor's edge and loving it.

"He's not even afraid," Johnson remarked.

Dob joined us, shaking his head. "That Frenchman's a fool." But he didn't look away, none of us could.

We all held our breath while Roget planted the bundle of dynamite and lit the fuse. Then, he frantically waved his arms for the men to swing him up.

Before I could see if he was clear, there was a huge explosion, white water and logs blasted out of the center of the jam. In the confusion, we lost sight of Roget. But that mountain range of logs was moving. A hooping and a hollering went up from both sides of the river.

A few minutes passed, and me and the other fellas ran down along the riverbank, looking to see if he'd made it.

Then, I saw Roget being pulled from the river. His body was all beat up and bloody, and he was holding his side, but he was grinning like a kid on Christmas morning.

We all rushed over to him, congratulating him and patting him on the back.

"You did it! You did it!" I shouted. The next moment, I felt foolish for calling out knowing that Roget didn't think much of me.

"Sevy, she blew high." He clapped me on the back as if we were good friends, then accepted more congratulations from Johnson, Dob, and the others.

I grinned back at him like a fool. Because, despite everything, in that moment, Fabien Roget was again my hero.

I think that all of us from the Daniel Shaw Company were walking a little taller that afternoon. After all, one of ours had blown the jam.

Chapter Thirteen
~ Going Home ~

The remaining days of the river drive passed in a blur of freezing water, mugs of hot tar, and pure dog tiredness, but I didn't want it to end. Near every day, I practiced burling and learned my feet could fly. But each bend of the river brought me closer to home, to Eau Claire, and I wasn't sure how I felt about that. Sure, I wanted to go home, but I also wanted to keep being the person I was now, a lumberjack and a river rat. I didn't want to go back to being just a schoolboy. I'd experienced too much to fit back into my old life.

On the day that we arrived in Eau Claire, the logs went through the flumes into Half Moon Bay. Then, we sorted the logs by company. I kept looking up to see if any of my family had come for me. It was near the noon hour, and I was standing on a log, sorting through others by their marks, when I glanced over on the shore and saw some folks standing there watching us. Leaning on my peavey, I squinted my eyes against the bright afternoon sun. I saw it was my pa, brother and sister all standing up there waving down at me.

Peter and Marta were jumping up and down, but Pa just waved and waited, like he had all the time in the world. Ma wasn't there.

Dob saw them, too. And he saw me looking up at them. "Boy, go on up to them. We won't get this job done tonight. Me and the boys are going to call it quits for the day soon enough. We all have some celebrating to do."

So, I hightailed it out of there. I dropped my peavey on the shore, then hesitated, knowing a river rat never just leaves a good peavey laying around. When I turned to go back and get it, I saw Johan had picked it up.

He waved to me. "Go on, Sevy."

I walked quick 'til I knew that I was out of sight, then I ran as fast as I could up to my family.

Pa started walking down toward me when he saw me heading his way. Sure, he was favoring his leg a little, but he was whole and he was walking, near jogging even. When I got close to him, I slowed down.

"Hi, Pa." After a moment, I held my hand out to shake his.

His eyes looked bright. He stared at me. "You too grown up now to hug your Pa?"

I hesitated for only a moment before launching myself at him. He bear hugged me, then clapped me on the back.

"Pa..." A lump in my throat kept me from saying more. Sure, I'd hugged my Pa in public, but I still wasn't about to start bawling, too.

"Let me look at you, Sevy." Pa held me at arms length. "Well, you're thin, so your ma will say. But you've grown this winter. You're near as tall as I am. And thick, too. The winter agreed with you."

I nodded, too choked up to speak. It was odd being able to look him in the eye.

Then, Peter and Marta were on me. Marta was a hugging and a kissing on me while Peter tugged on my arm and asked a thousand questions.

Finally, Pa said, "Let's get going home, children. Your mother has planned a fine welcome for you, Sevy."

"How did you know I'd be here today?"

"We knew when the logs were coming in and we've been watching ever since."

We walked to the wagon that Pa had borrowed for the ride out to Shawtown. Marta and Peter kept a-jabbering away, so I didn't have to say much, which was good.

"Sevy," Pa said, touching my arm when I went to untie the brown nag pulling it. "I spoke with Joe Lynch and he said you did a fine job this winter. Your mother and I are proud of you, real proud of you."

"We have a surprise for you," Marta chanted, a grin on her face.

"Yessiree," Peter added.

I grinned back, and reached over and flipped up the brim of his cap. "Aw, come on and tell me. You never could keep a secret."

"I can, too," he answered.

"No, you can't, Peter." Marta stuck her tongue out at him. "You know you can't, which is why I told Ma that you shouldn't come today."

"You'll hold your tongue this time, Peter." Pa glowered, but his voice lacked its usual weight.

Whatever the surprise was, they clearly expected me to be

pleased with it. So, I didn't say a thing. I just looked down at the ground and scuffed my toe in the dirt while Pa climbed up into the driver's seat. He moved real gingerly, and he shook a little bit when his weight went on the leg. It worried me some. I couldn't see him lumberjacking again moving as he was now. Once he was on board, the rest of us scrambled up and I sat right next to Pa.

Riding through town and over the bridge felt strange. Eau Claire looked real normal, like it always had. The sawdust-covered muddy streets, the pine-board sidewalks, the saloons, shops and houses, all of it was the same. But I had changed. Could folks see that? Would anyone be able to tell? How would it feel to be just a schoolboy again?

In no time at all, we were heading up our street and then I saw our house. There were folks spilling out of the little whitewashed building and gathered in the tiny yard beside it.

My jaw dropped. "Pa?"

"Yes?"

"Why are those folks there?"

"To welcome you home."

"That's your surprise," Marta put in.

"Why isn't anyone working today?"

"It's Saturday." Peter rolled his eyes.

I'd lost track of the days during the river run. We'd arrived in Eau Claire on a Saturday.

Then, I saw my Ma. She stood right in front of everyone else. She looked the way she always had, with a smile that warmed me from the inside out. Wearing her church dress, she still had an apron on, which she used to dry her hands. She ran towards us. I jumped off that still moving wagon, and then she was holding me, hugging me. She smelled so good and familiar and for the first time since leaving the Northwoods, I felt peaceful about being home.

"Oh, Sevy." She grasped my shoulders and looked me up and down. "You've grown. And to think I used to carry you everywhere with me. Look how long your hair has gotten." She touched my hair and I pulled back.

"Ma," I muttered, rolling my eyes, very aware that there were people all around us.

"Yes, well, you are so grown up now." Her brown eyes were bright with unshed tears, but she smoothed her dress and took my arm. "You have a lot of friends here to see you today."

"How did you get everyone here? I mean, I didn't even know what day we'd be getting into Eau Claire."

"We heard you were likely coming in today. Jeremiah Ritter saw you down at Half Moon, and he brought us word. Then Marta, Peter, and Hugh went around and told folks we were having a get together. Folks began stopping by, lots of them, all bringing something."

She led me into the little yard where we greeted neighbors, my pa's friends from the mill, and some friends from school, and even Mr. Watters.

"You'll have to tell me all about your adventures up north," Watters said. "I hope that you conducted yourself well."

"Of course my son did." My mother bristled. "Sevy's a good boy and a hard worker."

Sure, she was defending me, but I'd gotten used to standing up for myself and now I felt about ten years old.

"I hope to hear about your adventures," Watters said. "It will be the closest I'll ever getting to working the pine, as they say."

But I didn't say yes or no.

Watters seemed to take my cue. "Well then, Sevy, Mrs. Andersen." He nodded to my mother and moved away.

"You help yourself to something to eat. That's Mrs. Olson with one of her pies. I'll be right back." She bustled off while I eyeballed the grub that was already out on our table. Ma and the other ladies had laid out quite a spread even with the short notice. My mouth was watering. Then, someone grabbed me from behind and spun me around. Immediately, I ducked and got ready to come up fighting, but found myself staring right at Hugh's flushed face and bright red hair. He was even taller, skinnier, and more red headed than when I'd last seen him.

"Hugh." I couldn't help grinning back. Hugh had that effect on a person.

"You missed a lot of fun this winter, Sevy. But you're back now and everything will be like it used to be."

Would it? I felt downright peculiar.

Hugh leaned close, his blue eyes bright with excitement. "She's here."

"Who?"

"Adelaide Jaeger. She came with my sister. They're over on the other side of the house.

We ambled outside all casual like and there I glimpsed Hugh's sister Margaret and with her, sure enough, was a girl with a familiar long blond braid. Adeleide. Suddenly, she turned, saw me, and smiled. At me. Right at me! Out there, in the sunlight, she looked as pretty as a picture. I didn't realize I'd been staring until I saw her blush. We both turned away at the same time.

"She's asked me about you a couple of times this winter. You gonna talk to her?"

I couldn't keep up with him. It was all too much to take in. Adelaide may very well have come to see me, but I didn't know what to say to her, and having thought about her all winter sure didn't help.

Still I let Hugh drag me over to the two girls. Before I knew what was what, I was standing right in front of her and she was looking at me.

"Here he is," Hugh announced.

I glared at him.

He cocked an eyebrow at me.

"Hello, Sevy," Adelaide said, her voice soft and sweet, just like I'd remembered it.

"Adelaide." I nodded like Mr. Waters had. "How's your pa?"

"He's just fine, thanks for asking."

"How's school?" I wanted to think of something interesting to say, anything at all, but I couldn't come up with a thing.

"Good," she said. Then, we both stood there and stared at each other. I couldn't think of a thing to say.

"Sevy, I want to hear all about what it's like, lumberjacking and running the river. All of it. Did you get hurt? We heard a couple of fellas drowned during the river run this year. Were you scared?" He didn't pause, even to take a breath.

With Adelaide's eyes on me, I started to sweat. "Uh, there ain't much to tell."

"Come on, Sevy. I want to hear about everything."

I saw Margaret roll her eyes at Adelaide, but still I couldn't think of anything smart or interestin' to say.

Then, Margaret waved to someone in the crowd. "There's Ellie. Come on, Addie. Bye boys. Hugh don't forget to check on Owen," she said, referring to their younger brother before tugging the other girl away.

I saw Adelaide steal a glance back at me.

"Were you scared much?" Hugh asked.

"What? Nah. She's just a girl."

"Not by Adelaide, by lumberjacking." He smacked me on the back of the head. "Did you hear the news about the burling contest? There's going to be one down on Half Moon tomorrow afternoon, when we're all done with church going. I heard that the lumber companies put up the prize. A hundred dollars! I'm thinking of trying myself, and I ain't ever learned how."

He kept rattling on, but I wasn't listening. A hundred dollars! If I won it, Pa might not have to go lumberjacking next winter. If we were lucky, maybe we'd finally have enough with what my folks had already saved to buy a farm of our own.

I could see it all: me, winning the prize, and everyone being there to see it. Maybe even Adelaide. She may even get so excited that she'd hug me or give me a kiss.

"A hundred dollars?" I repeated. "For a burling contest?" It didn't seem possible.

"Yup. I told you," Hugh nodded triumphantly, excited to share the big news. "The lumber companies are putting up the money. Now that the logs are in and the jacks are here, the whole town's celebrating."

Every year, when the log run was finished, folks let loose in Eau Claire. With the lumberjacks in town with money in their pockets, the saloons stayed open late into the night and streets were filled with folks during the day.

"What are you boys up to?" I felt a familiar hand on my shoulder as my pa came up.

"I was telling Sevy about the big burling contest on Half Moon Lake."

Pa nodded, amused by Hugh's excitement. "The bosses think that the contest will be a good way to keep the tensions down between the companies. They don't want any trouble this year. It's a winner take all event. You know of any good burlers from your outfit? Someone I should put some money on."

Immediately, I thought of one particular jack. But he wouldn't be likely to enter a burling contest, would he?

"I sure do, Pa. Put your money on me."

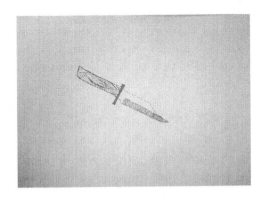

Chapter Fourteen
~ The Contest ~

The next morning, I was up before dawn. I was tired, but had been unable to fall asleep for much of the night.

Seeing me in my river rat gear, Ma just shook her head, a small smile pursing her lips. "Haven't you had enough of it yet?"

"Just this one last time, Ma. Then it'll all be over with. You'll come watch, won't you?"

"Of course." She hugged me tight. She smelled like oatmeal and brown sugar and it felt good to be home.

In was near sunrise when Hugh and I got a ride down to Half Moon Lake on a milk delivery wagon.

It was still early enough in the morning that tendrils of steam were rising up off the lake. Men were already moving around on the lake's surface, sorting logs. A few town folk were moving around the lakeshore as well.

Hugh was uncharacteristically quiet, which was just fine with me, because I was looking for my crew. We found them soon enough. The Push, Dob, the Swedish brothers, Bob Johnson and Roget were all there.

"Sevy," Dob greeted me. "Did they manage to beat city back into you?"

"What?" I asked. That fella did say the oddest things. I jerked a thumb at Hugh. "This here's my buddy, Hugh McLean."

"We're here for the burling contest. Sevy's gonna compete."

Dob glanced over at me, his eyes sharp.

I nodded.

The fellas began to swarm around me, talking a mile a minute.

"You think you can beat me?" Ole asked thumping his chest. "How do you like that, Johan? The student tries to beat the teacher."

"Who are you kidding, Ole?" Bob Johnson snorted. "It'll be a miracle if you can even get up on that there log after last night."

"I'll beat you both," Johan announced.

"I'll leave you young roosters to sort things out. I haven't had any breakfast yet. I could use a stack of flappers and some black lead. Anyone want to join me?"

So, Dob headed off, and Johan and Ole went to register for the burling contest. I had to register, too, but everything was happening so fast that I wanted to catch my breath. I told Hugh and the other fellas I'd be down in a minute.

I looked down over that log filled lake, thinking about how I'd helped fell some of them. The logs were so thick in the water that I wondered if I could walk across the lake on them from shore to shore. It seemed impossible now that I was back that all of it, my winter in the Northwoods, had really happened.

"We did well this year."

I turned. Roget had appeared right beside me, looking down at the logs. "It was a good season."

"Sure was."

He looked right at me and, for the first time, I realized I could look him in the eye. I was now as tall as he was. He'd seemed like a giant to me when I'd first gotten to camp.

"You been paid?" he asked.

"No." I shook my head. "I ain't gone down to the office yet."

He nodded. "Make sure they don't cheat you. You did a man's work this winter. I'll talk to the Push and make sure that the company pays you right."

"Thanks."

Still, he stared at me, obviously wanting to say something else.

"You'll go back to school now?"

"Yeah, I guess so." I exhaled slowly. Going back to school. It seemed like another life. "Well, maybe I'll see you up north some time."

"*Non.*" Roget looked at me real intent. "You don't go back. You are not one of us and never will be. I will talk to your father." With that, he turned on his hewl and walked away.

I didn't say a thing, just stood there and took it. I was finally done trying to prove myself to Fabien Roget. You can't fix what's wrong with other folks, as my ma always said. Besides, it was time to go and sign up for the burling contest.

It was all set up right at Half Moon Beach. Not far off the shore, a big, thick, near twenty-inch pine log floated in a roped off area where I guessed the water was more than waist deep. Though it was real early yet, folks were already moving around. When I went and gave an official my name, I peeked over the fella's shoulder and saw that a lot of jacks were already entered. It shouldn't of surprised me. After all, a hundred dollars was at stake, a fortune for men who earned a dollar a day risking their lives in freezing conditions all winter long.

After taking care of business, I wandered around. The beach felt like the county fair. By midmorning, just before the contest got started, my folks found me. I waited with Pa and Peter for my turn.

A burling contest worked like this: you had two men, each standing and facing different directions on a log. Each tried to get that log turning, rolling it in the water, so that the other fella couldn't keep up and fell off into the sink. A good burler could speed a log roll up or slow it down, or even make it change directions.

In the first rounds, I was lucky. My first draw was against a thickset fella from the Knapp and Sons Lumber Company. He was steady, but had slow feet, and I had him off the log lickety split.

Next, I went up against a Danish fella, and he was tougher to shake. He could go fast, but he lost his balance on a direction change.

By my third go round, I was feeling cocky. People were starting to shout my name when it was my turn to wade out into the cold water of Half Moon Bay to belly up on a log.

One man yelled, "I got money riding on you, boy. Don't let

me down."

And sure enough, I didn't. For once, it seemed like things were going smooth for me, like I could do nothing wrong.

I watched some of the other fellas have their goes. There were a few who worried me: a German fella with tiny feet who seemed glued to the log, an Ojibwe Indian who was so smooth, he barely looked like he was moving up there, and Roget, of course. But I didn't watch his rounds.

By midafternoon, they were down to the final twenty jacks. Womenfolk brought food down to the beach. The whole thing was beginning to feel like a party, and I kept winning. I wouldn't have said that I was better than those other fellas, because I wasn't. Many were far more experienced burlers, but somehow the rounds kept going in my favor.

"Young legs," I heard one jack mutter as he sloshed his way out of the lake after coming off. By afternoon, I knew that I had made the finals. I didn't know who I would be up against. The final rounds weren't set to start for another hour, so that the judges could get a bite to eat. The folks and excitement were getting to be too much for me. So, Hugh and I moseyed down the beach a piece. I sat on a stump and looked out over the still water of the little bay. Closing my eyes, I tried to remember how it had felt burling in the backwaters, the quiet, my feet flying, my body still. The not worrying, because no one was watching part.

"Nah, Adelaide. Sevy doesn't want to talk right now. He's resting up for the finals."

My eyes flew open.

"Just tell him... Tell him that I wanted to wish him luck."

I don't know where the courage came from, but I opened my eyes and said, "You can tell me yourself."

Adelaide and Kate, who was again with her, stood looking at me, but Hugh got the picture. He winked at me. "Come on, Kate, let's you and me have a look at that results board."

For once, she didn't argue back, and that left Adelaide and me standing there together and sorta alone. She was so pretty, and she was looking right at me. I glanced away, feeling sorta sick down in my stomach.

"This is for you." She held out a carefully folded bit of paper.

I reached out to take it from her and our fingers touched. I swear I felt a shock coming from her to me. But then she dropped her hand real fast, like she felt it, too. Thinking it was a note, I began to unfold it.

"Be careful, you'll drop it."

I slowly opened that paper out the rest of the way and found a dried and flattened bit of plant in it. I looked up at her.

"It's a four-leafed clover."

I looked more closely at it, and, sure enough, it was. We'd searched for them in the schoolyard when we were younger, but I'd never seen a real one before.

"I found that one last summer."

"And you're giving it to me?"

She glanced back up at me and her eyes were keen. "Now don't you go getting a swelled head, Sevy Andersen. I've found others before. In fact, I have a whole box of them at home. Margaret says that they bring good luck."

I don't know what got into me, but then as bold as brass, I said, "But have you ever given one to a fella before?"

Of course, that made her blush. She turned, like she was

111

gonna to walk away.

"It was real nice of you to give it to me."

Suddenly, I knew that this was one of those times where you have to man up or regret it forever after. I folded that bit of paper back up. "Thank you, Addie." Now, my heart was pounding fit to pop out of my chest, but I reached out and took her hand and I held onto it. Somehow words came to me. "I'll keep it. Not on me during the contest, in case I end up in the drink, but in my jacket on the shore."

"You won't. End up in the water, I mean." Her eyes were bright and warm and on me and I was aware of her down to the tips of my toes.

"Hey, Sevy." Hugh was back now and running up to us. Adelaide dropped my hand. "I know who the other finalist is."

"I have to go. Find my pa, I mean." She turned on her heel and high tailed it out of there. I watched her link up arms with Kate and then start whispering to her the way that girls do.

"What did she want?" Hugh asked gesturing at her with his thumb.

"To wish me luck." He didn't need to know about the four-leafed clover.

He snorted. "Well, you're going to need it. It's you and that Roget fella. I heard folks talking and they say he's really good, likely, the best in these parts."

I groaned and tugged my fingers through my hair. *Why did it have to be him?*

"Well, is he as good as they say?" Hugh demanded, pulling my hands away from my face. You woulda thought he stood a chance to win a hundred dollars.

"Yup, he sure is. And then some."

* * * *

It was near sunset by the time Roget and I stood side by side on the beach eyeing the log. It was getting cooler now and I shivered in the evening breeze that was coming up off the lake. Folks were gathering around the bonfires that had been built on the beach. Everyone looked like they were having a real good time, everyone, that is, but me.

I felt sick, not pukey sick, but bone cold and tired. I was tired from all of it, from the winter spent lumberjacking, from the river drive. I knew I wasn't gonna win. Roget was just plain better than I was and probably ever would be. All day long, I'd caught glimpses of my friends from the logging camp. Most of them had been cheering me on. I wondered who they'd be rooting for now. I closed my eyes, clearing my head.

While we waited standing there on the little beach, some big wig from one of the lumber companies that had put up the prize money gabbed on. I just wanted to get it over with. I closed my eyes, clearing my head.

"Sevy."

I opened my eyes.

"Sevy?" Roget said just loud enough so that only I could hear him.

"What?"

To my surprise, he held out his hand.

I stared at it. It was huge with black hair on the knuckles and scars that stood out against the tan of his skin. They were a real lumberjack's hands, big knuckled and scarred. I glanced down at my own hands, which were pale and unmarked, in comparison, but near as big.

"So, it comes down to us," he commented with one eyebrow arched. "You have done well to get this far." Still, he held his hand out to me, waiting

I exhaled slowly and then I took it, but not for him, for me. We shook. He gripped my hand hard, the way he probably gripped an axe handle. But I didn't give him any quarter.

"May the best man win," he said.

Hearing that, something sorta snapped inside me. He probably thought I had no chance, but I was done taking it.

I looked away from him and fixed my eyes on that thick log of white pine floating in the bay. Neither of us said another word. I wish I could paint a picture of how it was. There was a hint of the moon in the sky, the sunset was beginning to set but it was still bright enough to see. The water was smooth and dark.

When that lumber company fella was done chatting up the crowd, we waded out into the icy water, moving slowly to the log. At a signal from an official, we both bellied up to it, from opposite sides. Now, Roget sized me up. But I eyeballed him right back and we waited.

The eerie cry of a loon broke the stillness.

"Gentlemen, are you ready?" the official called from the shore.

Moving slowly and carefully, the way I'd done in the backwaters of the Chippewa, I turned and stood. Roget did, too, though we were facing in opposite directions. I could hear someone breathing real loud, then I realized it was me.

There was a gunshot, the signal to begin, and I stopped thinking.

Roget moved first and I just followed the roll of the log. My knees were bent, my feet, light, my arms, extended out to help balance me. Despite the pounding of my heart, I forced my breathing to be slow and controlled. Burling was about rhythm and control. It wasn't about going as fast as you can; it was about staying within yourself and not fighting either the motion of the log or of the other man.

As we rolled the log, ripples began to move out from it. And, to my amazement, I wasn't running or fighting for balance. I wasn't even afraid of losing. I was dancing. My legs were moving smoothly and easily, and I felt like I could keep on forever. My balance was as good as if I was walking down the center of Barstow Street. I laughed out loud.

"Eh boy, let's see what you got." Roget took my laugh as a challenge.

"Fine, old man," I taunted.

He grinned back at me.

Now I made my feet fly, forcing the speed of the turning log faster. Roget kept pace, as I'd known he would.

After a few moments, I felt some resistance to the speed I was setting. Roget was slowing the log down. Using the strength in his legs, he suddenly forced it to turn in the opposite direction. Then, he pushed it faster and faster still. Then, he started mixing things up, giving me all he had, throwing in a lot of changes of direction, slowing down and speeding up. But I kept my eyes fixed on that log and I went with it. He controlled the motion of that log for several long minutes.

Sure, my legs were burning and my lungs were pumping like a bellows, but I knew he had to be hurting as well. It was then that I made my move. I forced my legs faster, pushing the speed back up.

Roget kept up with me. And now the duel began in earnest. Back and forth, each of us using our strength and balance to control the roll of that pine. Roget didn't hold back or go easy on me. He gave it all he had, and I took it and came back for more.

But I was flying. As if from a long distance, I heard people shouting, calling my name and Roget's. But I focused on my job, staying upright on that log. I could do it! I knew I could. He had to be tiring. I was going to win! I just knew it. Then, I looked up. For a second, I glimpsed my family, standing on the shore, waving and cheering.

It was then that I made my mistake. My right foot slipped, probably because I'd gotten distracted for just that second. I tried to catch myself, but I was tipping forward. Then, the oddest thing happened. In my panic, I looked over to Roget. He saw that I was in trouble, and then he slowed the speed of the log roll. He slowed that log so I could regain my balance. Now folks on the shore couldn't see it, but I knew what he'd done. He'd saved me.

We kept on, for a while longer, but the next thing that happened was even crazier yet. I felt that log slow down even more, and then Roget's arms began to wave, like he was losing his balance. Astonished, I watched as he slipped down into the water with a splash. And just like that, I'd won.

Folks were yelling and screaming as I slid in after him. I came up gasping against the cold water and I stared in astonishment at him. He was grinning and he raised two fingers to his forehead in a salute.

Someone plunged into the water beside me, grasped my hand, and held my arm up. "Our winner!" People were shouting and clapping, but I broke away and ran through the water after Roget.

I grabbed him by the shoulder and I spun him around. I gripped his shirt in both of my fists. "Dog-on-it! You let me win. That's cheating!"

Even though I was in his face and yelling at him, that fool Frenchman grinned at me, his teeth big and white against his black beard.

"You can't let me win. You can't just do that. I coulda beat you fair and square. This ain't the way it's supposed to go."

"Sevy, the best man won. It is as it should be."

Then, he just turned and walked away from me. Immediately, I was swallowed up by my family and other well-wishers. My pa pounded me on the back, as proud as could be. My brother and sister were all over me. Folks were congratulating me. I tried to tell them all that Roget had let me win, but no one listened.

In all the confusion, I didn't even see where Roget went to. I wanted to talk to him, to make sense of what he'd done and said. Turns out, those were the last words I'd ever hear him say.

We celebrated that night until late. Everyone was there, my family, friends, and most of the fellas from the camp. It was near dawn before things settled down.

A few days later, when I was sorting through my gear from the logging camp something heavy dropped to the floor. Thank goodness, it missed my feet. It was a knife and one I'd seen before. I reached down and picked it up. It was a Jim Bowe blasé, Roget's knife. He'd left it for me.

Final Thoughts

With the hundred dollars from the logrolling contest, my earnings, and the money my folks had saved up, we finally had enough money to buy a nice piece of land just outside of Eau Claire and a team of horses, too. Buying that land meant the world to Pa. He'd finally achieved his dream.

That summer we were real busy with planting and building. All of us kids had to pitch in. Pa was a hard worker, but the leg slowed him down some.

Even with the new farm, I went back to school that fall, and to my surprise, I found it tolerable. It was a heck of a lot easier than lumberjacking or setting up a farm.

With the first frost that fall, I felt an itchin' for the fresh cold air of the Northwoods. I saw jacks shopping for their gear, strutting through town, and I felt a hankering to be one of them again.

White Pine

Some folks say that the pine will run out one day, that lumbering is wasteful and that the way that we do it ruins the land. I've seen it with my own eyes and I'll be the first to admit that it's a shame to cut down those giants and leave nothin' but scrub in their places. This may sound crazy, but when you walk into virgin timber, it's like being in a church, and there isn't anything sadder than a cutaway.

I expect the great pines will be gone one day and so will the jacks who took them down. Those fellas, good or bad, were real and alive in a way that other folks just don't understand. When a cool wind blows out of the north, my heart still beats a little faster. I'll never forget Dob, Bart, the Push, the Swedish brothers, all the others and but especially not Fabien Roget. Other folks can come and go from your life, but you never forget legends.

THE END

Glossary of Terms

À bientôt — French, See you soon

amen corner--corner of a logging bunkhouse used for talking and storytelling

black tar — coffee

bluebacks — ticks

caulks — studs on a horse's shoes that provide traction

cookee — cook's helper

cootie cage — bunk

Dia duit — Irish Gaelic, God to you, a greeting

doorknobs — dinner rolls

Gabriel horn — four or five foot long horn used to call lumberjacks to the cookshack for meal times

graybacks — lice

kroppkakor — a Swedish potato dumpling in this case filled with salt pork

Sacré bleu — French, a cry of surprise or anger

snabbare — Swedish, faster

togs — clothes

toque — hat

union suit — one-piece long underwear suit generally made of red flannel

About the Author

Caroline Akervik has been an avid reader since the fourth grade when a nun named Sister Dorothy introduced her to the magical world of Narnia. Caroline read anything and everything and was a particular fan of Marguerite Henry's horse stories and, especially, of King of the Wind.

Most of her early adulthood was spent as a professional horsewoman. She competed through the Grand Prix level of Dressage and worked with and trained many horses. Then, Caroline was blessed with a wonderful husband and three incredible children. Spending time with her own children motivated her to return to school to become a library/media specialist.

Now, Caroline shares her love of story and of the magic and power of words with the children she teaches. In her own work, Caroline seeks to write from the heart and to transport her readers and give wings to their imaginations. Caroline writes for young people, but agrees with C.S. Lewis that "A children's story that can only be enjoyed by children is not a good children's story in the slightest."

Blog: http://carolineakervik.blogspot.com

Other books by the author with Melange

A Horse Named Viking

Made in the USA
Lexington, KY
09 February 2017